The Dollhouse Mystery

By

Ronna M. Bacon

Psalms 121:1 I will lift up mine eyes unto the hills, from whence cometh my help.

2 My help cometh from the Lord, which made heaven and earth.

The Holy Bible, King James Version Public Domain

Table of Contents

The nightmare that had haunted her for so many years, that had kept her from sleep, that had sent her pacing her house and then to the outdoors seeking relief, was back. She shuddered in her sleep as she sank deeper and deeper into it. It had been gone for so long, but was back. She couldn't awaken, couldn't rouse, couldn't escape the inevitable.

She watched as he searched through the papers scattered over the table in his library, sorting them into names and events. He finally found the one he was in search of and held it up, reading it through again in the dim light. Yes, this was the plan he had devised so many years ago. Time had come to put it into place. The woman he wanted to hurt was an adult now, no longer a child. Hurting her would hurt her father. He needed to pay for what he had done to him.

She felt the anger rose within him, causing him to drop the paper back onto the table, making him pace, his footsteps heavy on the dark hardwood floor, slightly quieter as he stepped across the lush, heavy rugs strategically placed through the room. She saw as he finally stood at one of the floor-to-ceiling windows and pulled back the heavy drapes, staring out into the dark night. Even the moon and stars were hiding from his black mood. He stood for quite a time before he turned back, yanking the drapes closed, and headed for the table, searching once more for papers and then heading for the large, heavy, wooden desk where he dropped down into the black leather chair. He liked the darkness of the furnishings of the room. To him, they suited his mood. To others, they suited the man he had become over the years. Her tears flowed down her face in her sleep, knowing what was coming and what would wake her up.

She saw as he reached for his phone, making the call that set into play his plans. He gave a coarse laugh when he finished. The plans would move forward and could not be stopped. Not even the authorities would ever understand fully what he was up to. Fear coursed through her sleeping body as she tried to rouse, to run from the depth of that very fear, but her body and mind refused to obey.

She looked over his shoulder as he pulled up a program on his computer, staring at the picture of the dollhouse he had taken so many years ago. The house he lived in now was an exact replica of it, even to the furnishings, many of which he had had custom made. She tossed and turned as she recognized the dollhouse. What was going on?

She stepped back as he rose again, stalking through his house, even though he couldn't see her. He lived alone with just his wife, staff coming in to clean and prepare their meals. His secretary worked out of his business address and had never been to his home. His bodyguards were there, outside, to protect him from unwanted visitors. He didn't need them inside.

Hands to her mouth, she saw herself watching him as he stopped at a bedroom door and then flung it open, storming inside and staring around. Yes, he nodded, it was exactly as it should be. It was only a matter of time until the young woman was there, under his control. She would be his assistant, he decided, the lady on his arm at events, drawing even more unsuspecting men and women into his schemes, making him richer and richer. She would do what he ordered, the threats to her family would assure him of that.

She turned as the man's wife found him there, not sure of what he was up to, but too afraid to say anything. She was dying and knew she only had a short time to live. She had thought her life would be so different, she had been warned, and ignored the warnings. Now, she understood what her father had meant. She prayed that no one else fell under her husband's control but was afraid that was what would happen. The sleeper tried to reach out for help, but the woman ignored her.

The sleeper retreated in her dreams as he turned, shutting the room door, and almost shoving his wife out of his way. She had been useful when he first started out in business but had not supported him in later years. He ignored her looks of sorrow and pleas for him to stop what he was planning, slamming his own bedroom door after himself and turning the key in the lock in a loud manner.

The sleeper watched as the wife waited for him to return but he never did. She followed the woman as she walked down the stairs and out the door. She was done. If only she knew who it was he was planning to entrap in his business. She feared for those who came in contact with him, crossed his path. They would never survive, that she knew. He would beat them down and win.

Standing under the trees, the dreamer watched as the woman stared back at the house once more before she walked away. Her husband stood at the window and watched her leave, his mind already back on his plans and how to best implement them. The young woman he had focused on would never suspect him, he was sure. They all thought he was dead, had been for years. That was all part of his planning. He knew where she was, had searched her home numerous times, and knew who her friends and acquaintances were. Time had come, he thought.

The dreamer couldn't awake, couldn't escape the dream as it kept repeating itself, with subtle changes each time. Finally, she awoke, drenched in sweat, finding herself out on her back deck, her hands clenching tight to an upright post, barely keeping her from running from the house she adored. She leaned her head down on the post. When would it stop? And why now? Why had it returned?

Chapter 1

Cap slapping at his leg, Cameron Steele stared around his shop. Who had done this? Everything was tossed, wood splintered, paint and stain cans opened and poured out on the floor. He didn't dare move from the doorway where he stood, knowing he had to call the police, but still in enough shock that he couldn't move away from the door, or pull out his phone.

He turned and looked around him, knowing he had locked up tight when he had left the night before. This was not what he had expected to find nor what he really needed, not when he was working under a time crunch to meet his obligations. He sighed as he reached to place the cap back on his black curls, his brown eyes wounded but thoughtful. He pulled his phone out, his thumb running across the edge before he made a call he never ever expected to make.

Sitting on the picnic table he had under a tree, Cameron watched the activity of law enforcement officers working around and in his shop. He sighed. This was definitely a blow to him. He had clients who had expected to have their wood products and jewelry boxes ready for this weekend. It was

Wednesday and who knew when he would be able to start again. He had called his insurance company and they had expressed dismay for his situation and promised to send out an investigator. No, they told him, when he questioned this, an agent was not appropriate. Given what he had said, they wanted an investigator to take a look first and then they would decide from there.

He glanced up as he heard footsteps. His father sat beside him, a hand to his son's shoulder.

"What happened, Cameron? Your mom said you had called, looking for me." Cormac Steele stared towards the shop. "Something happen in there?"

Cameron snorted, drawing his father's eyes to his face. "What happened, Dad, did you ask? Someone destroyed my shop." His head dropped back down and he leaned forward, elbows on his knees, face buried in his hands. "Paint and stain poured out. Wood splintered. I didn't go in, so I don't know what all is damaged of the finished goods." He sighed, the sigh sounding as if it had been drawn from his toes up through his body.

His father sat, a hand on Cameron's back, the sound of nature in his ears, sun reflecting through the trees. He watched the activity much as Cameron had, turning his head as he heard a new vehicle approaching, a small SUV that he recognized. He frowned, his eyes dropping to Cameron. He didn't think Cameron had had an opportunity to meet the investigator that had just arrived, but he was concerned enough he knew he had to warn him.

"Cameron?"

"Yeah?" Cameron refused to look up.

"The investigator? Did they give a name?"

Cameron shook his head, defeat in the very motion. "No, just that they were sending someone. Why?"

"Because the investigator is here. Did you know Carrigan is the investigator?"

"Who?" Cameron turned his head to watch his father, whose eyes were in turn watching him.

"Carrigan Booth. Did you know Carrigan was an insurance investigator?"

Cameron shook his head. "You've lost me, Dad. I have no idea who that is."

Cormac shook his own head. "You might know her better as Carrie. She is younger than you by a couple of years, I think. Her family moved from here when you were about eight, I think.”

Cameron finally raised his head enough to stare towards the building, watching as a woman walked with an officer towards his shop, metal clipboard in her hand, before she stopped at the shop door, deep in conversation, he could tell.

“Sorry, Dad. I don’t remember her.”

Carrigan Booth shot a look around her, not sure why she was feeling so uncomfortable. She should be safe here, she thought, what with the officers still around. She listened as the responding officer explained what they had found and that the techs would soon be done. She nodded, having worked with them before. She stepped back, her stormy green eyes studying the building before she frowned.

“How did they get in?”

The officer shook his head. “That we’re still working on. Cameron said he had locked up everything last night when he left and had set the alarm. The alarm wires were cut, but for some reason, there was no warning sent to him like there should have been.”

“Someone tampered with the system?” She walked around the building, searching an entry point. "Nothing from the roof?" She stepped back to look up.

The officer shook his head. "We found no point-of-entry from the roof at all. The only thing...." He turned to watch Cameron for a moment and then turned back. "One of the tech thought the back window had been raised and lowered. She found splinters of wood outside."

"Show me." Carrigan stood for a moment before pulling out her camera. "I know you've taken photos, but I need my own. Can I approach the window?" At his nod, she cautiously stepped forward, camera pointed at the ground and then at the window as she took photos, before she leaned closer to the window. "Your tech's good. This is how they got in. This is an old window, easy to jimmy open." She pulled out her portfolio and began to jot notes. "He's never replaced the windows?"

"No. I have no idea why." The officer stopped, shooting a glance back at Cameron. "Cameron's a good friend of mine. He likely never thought what he did would draw in anyone to destroy it or maybe he just thought he had enough with the alarm system."

"He's got a good system. Systems work well when they're not tampered with.

That's something we'll be looking into, as I'm sure you are." She stepped back from the building, her eyes on Cameron and his father. "Is that Cormac Steele?"

The officer, Tim Black, shot her a look. "It is. Do you know him?"

She shook her head. "I used to live here, until I was eight and we moved. I can remember seeing him around church."

She sighed, her eyes back on her notes. "Can I go inside now or do I need to wait?"

Tim studied her for a moment. "You should be able to. Cameron will want to speak with you."

"I know he will. I just don't like this. Something's off and I can't figure out what or who."

"It's not Cameron. That I can tell you. He's as honest as they come."

"I'm sure he is. I have a job to do, and I will do it to the best of my ability." She walked away, her dark blond hair she had braided swinging behind her as she turned.

She stood finally, staring around, her notes and photos taken. She sighed. Such destruction, Lord, and for what? Who would do this? I know, I know. I need to talk to him, don't I? And that is something I'm not looking forward to. Most people are either defensive or offended when I approach them. I am tired of that, aren't I, Lord? But what option do I have? I need to find the truth here, no matter what it is.

She jumped as she heard a sound at the door and turned, hand to her throat as she swallowed hard. Lord, we need to work on this too, don't we?

Cameron stood there, just outside the door, his eyes searching the building before stopping on her, a frown on his face.

"Excuse me? You're the investigator from the insurance company?" His voice sounded hopeful.

"I am. Carrigan Booth." She walked towards him, forcing him to back away as she stepped outside, shutting the door behind her. "I need to ask you some questions, but first. Are you okay?"

He nodded. "I am. Just in shock and disbelief. I've worked hard for the last ten years to get where I am and now this." He ran his hand through his hair. "What do you need to know?"

"Give a moment to lock my camera away and then I'll be with you."

He nodded, a bleak look on his face as he studied first her and then the sun. "That's fine. I've lost today anyway to this. Can I get you anything? Dad's heading into the cafe for a meal for us."

She shook her head. "Thanks. I have some water with me. That's all I need."

He watched as she carefully locked her camera away as well as her metal portfolio, just keeping out a notebook and some other paperwork. He pointed to the picnic table. "How be we sit there? If that's okay?"

"It is." She finally sank down on the other side of the table, her papers in a neat pile in front of her. Her eyes thoughtful, she watched as he sat, his hands rubbing together, uncertainty on his face, devastation in his eyes. "It hurts, doesn't it?"

She began to ask her questions, noting his responses. He hesitated when she asked if he had any enemies or business rivals.

"Not that I know of." His comment finally came. "I'm sorry. I'm not much help."

She shrugged. "Sometimes we have enemies we don't know we have." She frowned as she heard a sound, standing to look around her and then the table. "I'm sorry. Did you hear that, Mr. Steele?"

"It's Cameron, and yes, I did. What is that?" He too had stood, searching under the table as they heard a low-pitched whining that grew louder and louder.

Carrigan spun, her eyes on his vehicle, and ran for hers, sliding to a stop as she heard the sound stopping, before she was behind the wheel of her SUV, spinning the wheel to pull it away from the building. She pulled to a stop and then jumped out, running towards Cameron as he spun in a circle, his eyes searching before they centred on his truck.

"It's coming from your truck, Cameron. What is going on?" Carrigan's hand reached out and pulled him backwards before he touched the vehicle. "No. Don't. Something is wrong."

"You're right, but the sound has moved. It's not from there now." He looked up, and gripped her arm, pulling her back towards the trees. "A drone! That's what we're hearing. Come on. Maybe we can make the trees."

Too late to reach the trees, he stopped and then pulled her away from them, running towards her vehicle.

A sudden sound stopped them in their tracks, their eyes on one another before they looked up at the drone almost overhead.

Cameron gave a shout and shoved her towards the ground as an explosion ripped through the ground and air, sending dirt and rocks towards them, peppering them. Cameron pushed her down, covering her as best he could with his body as another explosion sounded, this time close enough it shook their bodies and left them laying still, as the dust settled around them. After a few moments, the birds and insects began their songs in a tentative manner.

The drone hovered for a few moments and then sailed away, leaving almost a coarse laugh behind it in the sounds of its leaving.

Chapter 2

Carrigan moved under Cameron, shoving at him until she could slide away from him, his body falling limply back to the ground. Shaken, she sat up, eyes huge as she stared around. What had just happened, Lord? Are we safe, she questioned? She searched the sky, not seeing the drone, before she studied the debris and minor crevices in the ground in front of her. That was just too close, she thought. She spun to stare at the shop, seeing no damage there.

She reached out a hand to touch Cameron, seeing how shaky it was and froze. This can't be happening. Please, dear Lord. I came back here to be safe. I don't want to be selfish, but let that monster be miles away from here. Please, Lord?

She looked up again as she heard a vehicle brake suddenly, then the sounds of a door opening swiftly and running footsteps. A male dropped to his knees beside Cameron, hands reaching to assess him.

"What happened?" The words came out harsh. When she didn't answer, the man looked up. "I said, what happened? Why is Cameron out?"

20

She shook her head. "I...I...." Her voice died away as she stared first at him and then down at Cameron, who by this time was starting to stir. A hand on her back had her jumping and spinning to stare at Cormac Steele.

"Carrigan? What happened? Cameron said he was going to talk to you while I got us something to eat. Again, Carrigan?" He gave her a slight shake. "Carrigan. Snap out of it. What happened?"

She looked up at him before she spoke, her voice broken and shaking. "A drone. It dropped something, twice, that exploded. The second time it was too close to us. He shoved me down to protect me."

"A drone? Are you serious?" The man across from her stared at her, disbelief in his face.

She sprang to her feet. "A drone. Yes, a drone. Ask Cameron if you doubt me so much." Anger sparked from her as she walked rapidly to the table and gathered her papers and then to her vehicle, heading away from the shop.

"Corbin! That was uncalled for!" Cormac scolded his oldest son who still knelt beside Cameron. "She was here as an insurance investigator. Now, let's just hope you haven't alienated her and made things worse for Cameron." He reached down a hand to help Cameron sit up, before he felt around his son's head, stopping as he found the sore spot and Cameron ducked and pushed his hand away.

"Enough, Dad. I'll live. I've been hit worse." He turned to stare at his shop. "That's what I need to get at."

He pulled himself to his feet, staggered for a moment, and then headed to open his shop door, finally stepping through for the first time that day. He stared around, disheartened at what he saw, until he walked to where his completed work was sitting. He breathed a sigh of relief. His work didn't seem to be touched but he would need to go over each one and that would take hours, he knew. At least God was there for that, he thought.

He turned as he heard his brother coming towards him.

"Cameron? Who?"

Cameron shrugged. "I have no idea. Do you?"

Corbin shook his head as he reached to pick up a small chest. "No. I don't know of anyone who would do this to you. These are okay?" He set the chest back in its place.

Cameron nodded. "It looks as if they are. I'll need to go over them."

Corbin turned for a moment, surveying the shop. "I called in some reinforcements. Caitlin will be here with the crew shortly and they'll get to work cleaning. You can concentrate on this. I'll help Caitlin and her crew. Listen, I'm sorry. I think I may have offended your investigator."

Cameron's thoughts were on his work. "Who?"

Corbin shook his head. "Nothing." He turned as he heard his father call to them. "Dad's gotten a meal for us. We need to eat." As Cameron stood, not moving, his brother dragged him away. "Let's eat. Then we'll get to work."

Carrigan's hands were still shaking as she tried to unlock her house door. She paused, praying for peace and safety before she tried again, this time unlocking the door and shoving it open. She searched her house, knowing it was unlikely someone had been there, but she still didn't feel safe.

She finally set her camera and metal portfolio on the desk in her office, turning to head for the bedroom. She needed a shower, she decided, and clean clothes before she started. She heard the doorbell and ignored it, knowing that if it was someone who really wanted to talk to her, they would have sent a text that they were coming over. This is what she insisted on.

The knocks began and she hesitated, reaching for her phone and the app that showed the front door. She frowned. Cormac Steele stood there. Why? She finally walked to the door, hesitated to pray for strength and wisdom, and unlocked it, staring at the older man as he searched her face.

"Carrigan? Can I come in?"

She finally stepped backwards. "Sure. I apologize. I shouldn't have walked away like I did. I just couldn't stay." The hurt and fear in her eyes and on her face stopped him for a moment before he closed the door.

Lord, I have no idea what's going on here with this young lady, but You do. Let me speak with wisdom, please, dear Lord.

"That is okay. Cameron is fine. Corbin was out of line and I guarantee he will find you and apologize. Those two boys are closer than most brothers, always have been. Now, about you? Are you okay?"

She nodded, pointing to the kitchen. "I was just going to make some tea, or would you prefer coffee?"

"Nothing for me, thanks. I just wanted to make sure you were okay and reassure you that Cameron is. I need to head back there to help with the clean up. My daughter works for a commercial cleaning company and she's sending out a crew to help. It will be a long night but we'll have him back up tomorrow."

She nodded, a frown on her face. "Wait. There was something I needed to ask Cameron about and didn't get a chance. Maybe you can tell me." She headed for her camera and came back to him, flipping through the pictures until she found the one she wanted. "I found this on the work bench. It just didn't seem to fit."

Cormac studied the object. "I've never seen that before. Maybe whoever it was dropped it. I'll ask Cameron."

"No, it is better if I do. You said you'd be there all night?"

"More than likely. By the time we clean up and sort through what's left, it will take a good portion of the night."

She nodded. "I'll head back there later. I need to work on my report and I'm sure I'll have more questions for Cameron."

She leaned back against the door after she had locked it tight again. Her head back, her eyes closed, she drew deep breaths. She shouldn't have been assigned to this case, she knew that only too well. It was a big case, and she was one of the newest in the office, well qualified, sure, but still the new one. So, why had it been given to her? That she might never know, but she had an uneasy feeling about it.

Cameron looked up from where he was sorting through the piles of debris, finding pieces of wood that he could use. It wasn't quite as bad as he thought initially. His tools and small supplies hadn't been touched. Just the stain and the paint, and the wood. Why, he thought? I don't compete with anyone here. I know my reputation is spreading for small handcrafted boxes and containers, but who would do this? Lord, I may never know. I'm not too sure about that investigator they sent. Dad seems to think she'll do all right, but this is my livelihood. I guess this is where you would tell me to trust, right, Lord?

He stood as he saw Carrigan walking towards him, a hesitation in her step that hadn't been there earlier. He knew Corbin had found them and sighed. Corbin, what did you say?

"Carrigan? Do I need to apologize for Corbin?" He waited for her to speak.

She finally shook her head, her eyes on him. "No, your father has already. Corbin is the one who needs to address that, not you, not your father. Are you okay? You were still not totally awake when I left. And I shouldn't have." She shook her head as he went to protest. "No, I shouldn't have. I left the scene of a crime, during an investigation. That's grounds to be removed from this investigation."

Cameron stared at her. "You're serious, aren't you? We won't let it happen. We know your employer well. He's my uncle. We'll make sure you stay on this."

It was her turn to stare at him. "I never made the connection. Your mother's brother?"

"No, my Dad's brother-in-law. He put the best one on this, he said. We've talked to him about what happened. He's very concerned about you, but won't say why, other than to comment he wasn't surprised you left the way you did."

She closed her eyes as she breathed a sigh of relief. Now that she knew the reasoning, she felt better. Her eyes popped back open, and Cameron felt lost in their smoky green. "You're sure you're okay?"

He nodded, before he motioned towards the shop. "Come on in. It looks better than it did earlier. My family and friends have worked wonders already."

She shook her head. "No. I just wanted to apologize for running off."

"There's a reason you did. I would like to know why." He held up a hand as she shook her head. "No, not now. At some point, you will tell me."

She finally sighed. "Maybe. Listen. I found something on your work bench that seemed out of place. A small metal candlestick, similar to a game piece."

He frowned. "I don't recognize that. I don't have any small pieces like that. I never used them." He turned to look at the shop, his hand clamping around her arm and pulling her with him, despite her protests. "We haven't touched it yet. Show me."

She stared down at the spot. "It was right there. I promise. It was. I have the pictures to prove it." She pulled out her phone and searched through, finding the picture she wanted and handing him her phone. "There. That's what I found."

He stared at it before he looked at the bench and then at her. "I've never seen that before."

Cormac spoke from behind him. "A game piece? Can I see?" Cameron handed the phone to his father. "Now, this is interesting. Where did it go?"

"It was here. I know it was." Carrigan looked around. "I shut the door when I came out, Cameron. You saw me." She spun and then walked towards the back of the building, weaving among the workers, not catching the glances Corbin and Caitlin shot at her, angry on Corbin's part, questioning on Caitlin's. She pushed at the door and then took a good look at it, a sigh rising within her.

She turned and jumped, Cameron was that close behind her. "Next time, please, let me know you're there." Her hand to her throat, she stared at him, seeing the puzzled look on his face. "The door had been blocked. The latch. It's not catching. You can lock the door and think it's shut, but it's not. I don't remember seeing the lock on the door earlier when I was through with the police."

"I have no idea. I would have to ask Tim. Did you take pictures of it?"

She nodded. "And those are locked up tight."

"They are?" Cameron's question caught at the edge of her mind as she stood, eyes on the door, and then looking around before she stepped outside, her eyes narrowing as she studied the door and nodded. "Cameron? Does anyone have a key to this door?"

"Myself. My Dad. That's about it. Why?"

"Because I think this is how whoever it was got in. Not the window." She turned as she heard a sound of disbelief behind her and found Corbin watching her.

"You're with the police, are you?"

Cameron stalked towards his brother, standing between Carrigan and Corbin. "She's an insurance investigator and one of the best, I hear tell. Back off, Corbin." His words had a bite to them never before directed at Corbin, who jumped and stared at his brother, a frown in place. Cameron held up a hand. "No. Don't say another word. If that's what she says, then I believe her." He spun, his hand out to catch Carrigan's arm, and he led her back through the shop and outside to her SUV. "Can you show me what you have?"

She shook her head. "Not yet. I have to finish my report and put it in first." She sighed. "I know I'll be pulled off the case, having left like that."

Cameron grinned at her, his teeth white against the dark tan on his face. "Not a chance. I talked to your boss and he assures me you won't be pulled. He's not too happy someone tried to kill you and me."

"Is that what it was? An attempted assassination? You have strange friends and stranger enemies." She turned for her driver's door, stopping as he spoke quietly.

"No, I don't think I do. How about you, Carrigan? Do you have any enemies?"

She froze for a few seconds at his words and then without saying anything, climbed into her vehicle and drove off, leaving him standing, staring after her, his father walking towards him.

"Cameron? What's going on? Corbin looks like a thundercloud. You don't look much happier. This is not like either of you two."

"I know, Dad. Corbin doesn't like Carrigan, for some reason, and was not very nice to her. In fact, he almost accused her of not knowing what she's doing."

"And she does. Both of us know that. Corbin will once he realizes how good she is." He shot a glance over his shoulder, seeing Corbin standing about five feet behind them. "You two boys need to work this out.

Carrigan will be in our lives for the next while. I won't have you two sniping at each other. It's enough you were almost hurt by whatever that drone dropped, and with your shop the way it is, you have enough on your plate. You need Corbin's help." He turned Cameron to face Corbin. "I don't think I've ever had to tell you two boys to settle your differences. Not since you were toddlers. I will say it once and only once. Settle your differences. Work together. And Corbin, watch what you say. Your uncle has nothing but good to say about Carrigan. He's quite pleased with her. And you know how hard that is to have that from him."

Corbin watched their father walk away, disappointment showing at his sons, before he turned to Cameron, to find Cameron had turned back to watch where Carrigan had driven away.

"Cameron? I'm sorry. I didn't realize she was the investigator."

Cameron gave a clipped nod. "She is. She's good, too. She found something on the bench that's disappeared. A small metal candlestick that looks like an old-fashioned game token."

"What?" Corbin reached to pull Cameron back around to face him as he walked away. "A game token? Where have I heard that before in a crime scene?"

Cameron shrugged. He knew eventually Corbin would remember. Corbin was an investigative reporter, working freelance, and had access to documentation Cameron didn't have. "You have?" He shook his head. "Let's go back and see what we can accomplish before Mom arrives with the food." He groaned. "And now we have to deal with Mom."

Corbin started to laugh heartily at that. "Yep. Mom. What's your excuse this time?" He ducked the playful swat his brother aimed at him before he pulled him into a hug. "I'm so glad you weren't hurt any worse. Things can be replaced. You can't."

Cameron gave a nod as he studied his brother. "Thanks. God was looking after us today. That is a fact."

Chapter 3

Sorting through her paperwork, Carrigan sat back finally. She had finished her report, printed off copies of all the photographs she had taken, and was ready to head into the office to put in her report. She wasn't happy with it, though. Something was missing, and she just didn't know what.

She headed for her vehicle, stopping suddenly as something out of the ordinary caught her eye. She approached carefully. She wasn't seeing things, she realized. There was an envelope on the hood. She gingerly reached for it and then stopped. She spun in a circle, feeling eyes on her, and even looked up to see if the drone was back. It wasn't, but it didn't relieve her, that knowledge. Lord, what did I do? Did I bring trouble here with me? Or is this something new?

She pulled out her phone, knowing she had to be cautious but not wanting to make that call. It would dredge up the past, and the past was where she wanted the past to stay. She sighed. Even my thoughts are making sense, Lord, and to make sense is what I just want.

Tim watched Carrigan closely as he spoke with her before, with gloved hands, he reached for the envelope.

"You have no idea what's in it?" He eyed her face, seeing fear on it.

She shook her head. "No, no idea." She sighed. "You'll find out eventually, so I might as well tell you now. Four or five years ago, I witnessed a bank robbery and was able to identify one of the culprits. They never found the money or the accomplices but I received threatening mail, that told me if I talked any more I would be dead. I left that town and moved to another and then here about four months later. I have refused to go back to testify. They have had to rely on my statement, and no one has been happy about that." She looked up at Tim. "While I was still in that town, I would find envelopes like that on my vehicles, on my desk at work, in my mailbox. I have no idea if they have found me or not."

Tim nodded, his head bent once more over his notebook, seeing Cameron standing just behind Carrigan. "Cameron's here, Carrigan."

Her eyes slid shut. "Cameron? How? And why? He shouldn't be, you know?"

Tim nodded. "Let it go for now. Let's see what's in this." He carefully opened the envelope, surprised it had not been sealed shut and dumped out a small metal object. "A candlestick?"

"What?" She leaned closer. "That's the one I photographed on Cameron's work bench."

It was Tim's turn to stare at her. "What are you talking about? Our techs never said anything about this."

"Would they have known it didn't belong?" She countered, knowing Cameron had moved to stand beside her. "I asked Cameron. He said he's never seen it before."

"Carrigan is correct, Tim. I don't use things like that in my work. That's why it was a surprise when she showed me the photo. It was gone by the time she got back." He shared a look with her, seeing how stormy her eyes looked with the emotions running through her. "She also found that the back door had been tampered with. Did your techs find that?"

Tim stared at him and then shot Carrigan a look. "I have no idea. I'll need to talk to them. Why didn't you call me back?"

"Because there would have been no use, now would there?" Cameron felt his temper starting to rise and stepped back, a prayer for patience rising. "Sorry, Tim. This has gotten to me." He pointed to the metal object. "What's with that?"

Tim shook his head. "I'll take it in, but I doubt we'll find anything on it."

Carrigan nodded, her arms wrapped around her body as she too stepped back and then walked away. She needed to go to the office, but didn't know how she'd get there now. She glanced at her phone, seeing the time, and sighed. She jumped as she felt a hand on her arm.

"Sorry, Carrigan. I seem to have a habit of scaring you." Cameron's grin eased her fright. "You were heading somewhere?"

She nodded. "I need to head to the office to turn in my report. I can't use my vehicle and that sucks. Big time."

"Then, let me. I can run you there. Uncle Bill won't mind." He grinned as she shook her head, paused, and then nodded. "So, which is it? You're sending mixed signals there."

She shook a finger at him. "You have me confused. Let me grab my stuff." She headed for her house and unlocking the door, grabbed the file on the table just inside the door, locking the door behind her.

Cameron shut his truck door after her, turning as Tim approached for a quick word, before he slid behind the wheel. He gave a quick glance at Carrigan, seeing her sitting quietly, her eyes staring at her home, an unreadable look on her face, but he could see the fear in her eyes.

"Carrigan? Care to talk?"

She shook her head, not looking at him. "No. Once I drop this off, you need to walk away from me, Cameron. I'm a dangerous person to know. I don't want you or any of your family hurt because of me. I have to have a long talk with your uncle, it seems."

"Not on your own, you won't." Cameron shook a finger at her. "I'm staying."

"Cameron, this is not about you. It's about me and the danger I've brought here."

Cameron parked, then laid a hand on her arm. "Stay put until I open your door. But get one thing straight, I will stay when you talk to my uncle."

She stared at him, finally remembering to snap her mouth closed, and shoved the door open, and almost ran for the office, not hearing Cameron's quiet call after her.

She brushed past the receptionist who smiled and greeted her, looking for Bill Morrow, knowing she'd find him in his office. He waved her in and watched as she closed the door, a smile on his face as he heard Cameron's voice in the reception area.

"Trying to outrun Cameron?" He grinned at she nodded and sat.

"I am. He wanted to be in here when we spoke, and I won't have that." She handed over her report. "Here is my report. Basically the same as when we spoke earlier today. I've attached all the photos I took as well. I think you'll find the culprit came in the back door, not the window."

"That's what you said. You've done good work on this, I can tell you that already. You went about your work in a professional manner, not caring that it was a relative of mine that you were investigating. Most of the others here know Cameron and likely would not have gone into the details that you did. Thank you for that. This will help when whoever it is has been arrested." He shot her another look. "And no talk of moving on or being taken off this case." He sat back, his eyes on her. "We want you to stay in your home town. You need that. Trust Cameron with your secrets. He can help you."

Chapter 4

Three days later, Carrigan rose from her desk in her home office, heading for the kitchen and through it, to the back yard. She was still working through the final information on Cameron's investigation and was puzzled. Something was off about the whole thing, and she just didn't know what. She turned her face up to the sun, relishing the feel of the warmth on her face, hearing the sounds of the birds and insects in her ears, the sweet aroma from her flowers in her nostrils as she took a deep breath. She loved it here, but how long before she'd have to move? That she was afraid of. Having to pick up and move on. Start over in a new town. She loved this town, wanted to plant her roots back in her home town, but someone seemed determined to prevent that.

Her thoughts went to the parcel she had received that morning. It had no postmark. No return address. When she had cautiously opened it, the only thing in it was another game token, this time a thimble. What was the meaning of that, she wondered? Who was playing games with her?

She heard the sound of a doorbell and reached for her phone. She frowned as she stared down at the picture on her app. Why was Corbin Steele here? She didn't need to be interviewed by an investigative reporter, and a hostile one at that.

She finally moved through to the door, opening it a crack, leaving the screen door latched.

"What do you want?" Her voice sounded harsh, not like she wanted it to.

"Carrigan? I came to apologize and to talk to you. I need to. Please?" Corbin's demeanour was different from the last time she saw him.

"Why?"

"Because I remembered where I saw that token or something like it. And I need to see if you can help me."

She finally nodded, reaching to unlatch the screen and stepping back so he could enter. "Where's Cameron?"

"He's at work. I haven't talked to him yet." Corbin followed Carrigan to the kitchen, nodding as she held up the coffee pot. "Thank you. Listen. I really am sorry for the other day. Chalk it up to worry about

Cameron. I guess I've seen too much on my job."

"I guess you have. You need to learn to read people better, you know." She watched as he sipped at the coffee, not sitting as she expected, setting down the mug and pacing. "What is the problem, Corbin? What did you need to talk to me about anyway?"

He spun, coming to stand in front of her, staring down at her. "I found out where I saw the game token. It was from a bank robbery about five years ago." He held up a hand as she drew in a deep breath. "Sorry. I didn't mean it to come out like that. I'm better with pen and paper."

"I can find some for you, if you like." Corbin shot her an astonished glance, finally seeing the humour in her eyes she was trying to hide.

"You're a funny girl, aren't you? No. I think I can stumble through this." He paused, hand running through his dark brown hair. "Ten years ago, there was a bank robbed about four hundred miles from here. That was before the one I saw. They never got the culprits but they found a small metal game token on the floor. A candlestick, similar to what you found in Cameron's shop."

"And how do you think I can help?" She was suddenly afraid, knowing exactly where he was heading with this.

"I'm sorry. I don't mean to scare you or worry you. I've been keeping track of that investigation. A good friend was killed that day. An officer on the force. The same group has robbed other banks." He watched her closely, seeing how pale she had become. "Carrigan? Here. Sit. Where's your coffee? Here. Drink some. You're scaring me, you're so pale. What did I say?"

"Your friend? What town?" When he named the town, she paled even more, her hands shaking so much he reached to grip them, guiding them to the table so she could set down the mug.

"Carrigan? What's going on? Did you know him?"

She shook her head. "No, but I heard about him. Not from any news reports or police officers. I heard it from the robbers themselves."

He pulled out a chair, his eyes intent on hers. "What do you mean? You didn't live there. That's not what Dad said."

She shook her head, distress in her eyes. "No. I didn't. I'm sorry. I'm not able to talk about it, but I know they left something at each bank they robbed." She rose, walked across the room before she spun. "Don't say anything to anyone. If you do, they'll come after you. I know they will."

Corbin rose, a hand to his face, as he stared at her. "What do you mean?" When she said nothing, he stared at her, comprehension finally dawning. "I see. I guess that's why. You will need to talk to Cameron, won't you?"

She shook her head. "No. I don't think so. I need to talk to your uncle. I need to leave town."

Corbin's hand on her arm stopped her. "I think you've been running for too long, Carrigan. Talk to my uncle, but don't leave. Talk to Cameron. Whoever this is, he's in their line of sight in more ways than one. Don't walk away from him, please, if you can help him." He watched until she gave a reluctant nod, not looking at him. "You've been scared and that fear has now become terror. Let us help you. Let Cameron. He's already concerned enough he's talked to Dad about something. That something involves you. Neither would tell me why or what."

She finally nodded, her eyes unreadable as she looked at him. "I will talk to him, Corbin. But it will be my decision if I leave or not."

He turned to leave, seeing the thimble sitting on the table by the opened package. "Another one, Carrigan?" He spun back to face her. "Have you reported it?"

"What's to report?" She shot back. "There's nothing to identify the sender. I have no idea who it is or why me."

Corbin shook his head. "I think you do. And whatever or whoever it is, you've involved my family, without knowing. Whether it's related to what happened to Cameron, that remains to be seen. Just don't put my family in jeopardy."

"Don't threaten me, Corbin. I think that it is time you left." She followed him to the door, the screen door latched, and the locks on the wooden door after he left. She leaned her hands against it, her forehead tapping against it. He just had to show up, didn't he, Lord, and see that? How can I now avoid talking to Cameron? She turned to lean back against the door, her face buried in her hands, jumping as she heard her phone ring.

She walked towards the table, looking to see who had called her. Cameron. Now how did he get her number? Then, she shook her head. Her business card, of course. How had she forgotten? She glanced at the clock. He was likely still at his shop. She grabbed her phone and her keys, checked her license and debit card were in her phone case, and headed for her car, knowing she could not put off the inevitable any longer.

Cameron looked up as he heard the door to his shop opening, squinting at the clock. Almost closing time, he thought and sighed. Of course, a customer would come in at almost closing time on a Friday. He walked towards the door and stopped, a feeling of pleasure running through him. Carrigan stood there, her eyes looking everywhere but at him.

"Looks a little different?"

His voice caused her to jump and she spun towards him. "I thought we had come to an agreement. You weren't going to scare me any more."

He laughed as he walked the rest of the way towards her. "I'm sorry. I really have to stop doing that. To what do I owe the pleasure? And before you tell me, let me show you through the shop."

She followed him, seeing the differences in it. "You changed the layout."

"I did. This way is much better. The vandalism was a blessing in disguise, as my mother says. It forced me to change things around, just like she'd been after me to."

Carrigan laughed. "I can see that. Mom has done the same to me." She finally stood in front of his finished work, a finger tracing the carving on one of the boxes. "You are very good, I hope you know that."

He shrugged. "That's what I'm told. I don't see it that way. Just using the talents God gave me." He leaned one hip against the bench, his eyes assessing her. "Again, I have to ask. To what do I own the pleasure?"

She shook her head, and when she looked up, he saw the pain and sorrow in her eyes.

"Carrigan? What's going on?" He grasped her arm and led her to a seat, hunting for a bottle of water to hand her. "Talk to me. You're scaring me here, you know?"

She nodded. "I know I am. God knows what I have to say, and that doesn't make it any easier." She sighed, her hands on the bottle, her eyes on her hands. "I need to go back a bit, I guess."

"Start where you need to start." Cameron prayed for his new friend, not knowing exactly what she would be sharing.

She looked up finally at him. "Your uncle is the only one who knows the whole story. I think Corbin has guessed at some and likely researched me. He will not find out a lot, thankfully. That would put him at risk. What I am about to tell you will do the same."

Cameron reached for her hands, stilling the movement of them. "I don't care about that. What I care about is the stress you're under right now. You do not have to say a word, if that's what you want."

She bit at her lower lip, worrying it, before she shook her head. "No, I think….No, I do need to tell you. It seems as if somewhere our paths have crossed and whoever is sending me the letters and tokens has now decided to branch out to you."

He was puzzled, she could see, his brown eyes studying her as he thought through her words.

"Again, you do not have to talk to me. But if you do, please give me as much information as you can."

She nodded, her eyes growing large with fear. "I'm afraid, Cameron. I've been afraid for years that they will find me. I think they have. I've tried to hide. The detectives have tried to hide me. The crown prosecutors have tried to hide me. Yet, it appears they have found me."

"Who?   Who has found you, Carrigan?"

"The bank robbers from four, no, five years ago, I think. They've tracked me down and somehow connected me to you. And I don't know why." She buried her face into her hands even as Cameron's heart rose in prayer for her.

"Tell me, Carrigan. Tell me what happened and why you think someone has found you."

She finally nodded, a sigh wrung from her, pain on her face. "I will. It's not a pretty story, though."

"No, I don't think it will be. Tell me anyway."

Chapter 5

She finally spoke, her voice low enough that he had to lean close to hear her. He heard the fear, the panic, the distress in it and saw it on her face. His hands gripped her tight until she struggled to release hers, to turn them over and grip his again.

"It goes back four or five years, Cameron, and I'm not a liberty to say a whole lot. It's before the courts and that prohibits me from saying much." She looked up and he saw the tears she was fighting. He reached for her, to draw her to him, but she found his hands again and gripped them tighter, to prevent him from letting go. "Please, just let me talk. And don't interrupt. If you interrupt, I'll have to stop at whatever point we were at.

"Five years ago, I was walking towards my bank, on my lunch hour, to make a deposit when I heard shots and shouts and sobs. I froze, unable to move. Terror ran through me. I had no idea what was going on or if it was even in the bank or one of the other buildings. I heard running feet and dropped down behind a car, peeking out. I saw the men, Cameron, running from the bank. There were four of them. Only one didn't have a mask on. I saw him clearly. I think he saw me, because he stopped and his gun pointed at me. I ducked back and heard shooting. I couldn't move. I couldn't move. I froze right there. I heard running steps heading my way and prayed like I have never prayed before. Then I heard more shouts, commands, gunfire, and then the sound of the motor of their vehicle gunning as they sped away. I just stayed where I was.

"The police officers who responded found me. They made me stay right where I was, one officer with me, while they looked for the men and searched the bank. The robbers didn't kill anyone, at least not in that bank. They finally helped me to my feet and took me to their station. They called in the paramedics who said I wasn't hurt, at least not physically.

"I was the only one who saw the man. They did find him. Right now, the case is going through the courts. They have let me give a video statement that both the prosecutors and defence have agreed to let stand. There are others who may have seen him. I don't know. I have never asked.

"At the scene, they found a tiny metal object. The lead investigator asked me about it, but I have no idea why or what it was.

They haven't told me and I don't want to know."

She finally looked up at him, fearing that she would see censure and dislike on his face. Instead she saw concern for her and her safety and something else she wasn't quite sure about, admiration perhaps. She sighed to herself. *Not now, Lord. I can't handle someone else becoming interested in me, only to walk away when he decides I'm too dangerous to know.*

"Now, it seems as if his friends have found me. I can't stay. I can't bring trouble to you or your uncle."

Cameron's hands had never let go of hers even as she had tugged to release her own. His eyes on her face, he shook his head.

"Don't, Carrigan. Just stay put, please. I believe you when you say you're afraid. I would be too. That's a given. What I don't understand is how they would have found you."

"That's what I don't understand. I've talked to the lead investigator and he thinks someone has said something they shouldn't but he can't prove that or even figure out who would have. I'm sure he's done his best." Her eyes on his face, she sighed. "But how does that connect with you?"

"That's what we'll need to figure out. Did you say Corbin was digging into something?"

She nodded, her hair swinging against her face and she finally tugged one of her hands free to tuck the hair behind her ears. "That's what he said. He wanted information I think today from me but I can't say anything. I shouldn't have even talked to you." She blinked, her eyes sore from holding back the tears. "I talked to the lead investigator last night about something else, and mentioned what I had found. He didn't like that at all. He's heading this way to talk to both of us."

"And how does he plan on doing that without saying who he is?"

She shook her head. "I have no idea, but it won't be the first time we've done this, even here in town."

"He's been here before? Is that how they found you?"

She shook her head. "I don't think so. I think they've been searching the towns and found me that way. Unless someone is working for them on the inside." She stood, unable to sit any longer, and paced around the work area. She stopped, her finger running along a jewelry box. "You are so talented,

Cameron. How do you manage to carve the intricate work?"

He grinned as he came to stand beside her. "It's not hard. Just a matter of taking my time. I have great patterns that I trace onto the wood. They are all unique. I will only use a pattern once."

"That's so nice. There's nothing worse than finding out someone has the very same object you have." She turned, ready to head for the door, when his hand on her arm stopped her.

"Thank you, Carrigan. I know it must have been really difficult for you to tell me. I appreciate your confidence. But where do we go from here?"

"What do you mean? There is no we." She searched his face, not sure what he was meaning. "I'm going to talk to your uncle on Monday. After I talk to the lead investigator again, it will likely mean I'll have to move on."

"Not at all. Please. Don't move. Stay. Let us help you fight this." He played the one and only card he had to play. "I need you. You have to help solve what happened here and find the person responsible."

She shook her head. "That's not my responsibility, Cameron. That's the responsibility for the police. I have to leave it with them." She headed for the door, Cameron on her heels, his keys in his head as he hit the security pad to set the system, and then quickly locked up after her.

"Wait, Carrigan. At least let me buy you dinner or something."

She spun. "You don't have to do that. It's not necessary and not part of what I do."

He nodded, a grin on his face, mischief sparkling in his eyes. "Exactly. That's why I would like to take you out to dinner. Please? I'm grovelling here, in case you didn't notice." He kept grinning.

She finally shook her head. "Quit grovelling. It doesn't suit you. All right. One meal and one meal only. Is that a deal?"

He held up his hands. "One meal only tonight." He grinned as she frowned at him. "Really. Only one meal tonight. I don't think we could eat more than one a piece."

She sighed, knowing just what he was up to. "It won't work, Cameron. You can't bribe me to stay with taking me out to dinner."

He reached to tuck her hand into the crook of his elbow. "Then let me escort you to your vehicle. Follow me and I'll lead you to the best restaurant in town."

She looked around as he seated her at a table near the back of the restaurant, recognizing his family seated not too far from him. "This feels like a set up." She was grumpy and knew it.

"Not at all. This just happens to be a favourite spot of ours." He grinned as she shook a finger at him. "Besides, Mom's sister owns it."

"Now I know the real reason. You get free food."

He pretended to be shocked at her words. "Free food? Not at all. We pay for our meals."

"But at a family discount." His aunt stood at his side, bending to accept his kiss to her cheek. "Carrigan, you don't come in here often enough."

"I don't think I have. I would have, had I known it was your restaurant."

Placing their orders, Carrigan sat back, her eyes studying the restaurant, Cameron's eyes studying her. She looked back to find him watching her.

"Cameron?"

He shook his head. "Sorry. I was just thinking."

"Then think about something else. I don't like being stared at."

He laughed. "Was that what I was doing? I apologize. Then, tell me how come your parents moved."

She shrugged. "I have no idea. They just decided to move one day. No one ever really said why."

Their main course finished, Carrigan sat back, her eyes on the table, not quite sure how to tell him once again she had to leave. She sighed to herself. Lord, how do I do this? How do I walk away when I know someone's after him as well? She started as a hand reached to place a plate in front of her.

"I didn't order dessert." She stared down at the cheesecake sitting in front of her.

"Neither of us did, but Aunt Angela knew I would want her pineapple cheese cake. It's one of her specialities that she doesn't make very often."

She tasted it, nodding at the flavour. "I like this." She finished her piece and then sat back. "Cameron, we really do need to talk."

"I know we do. Just not tonight. Please? I'm out to dinner with a beautiful lady and I don't want business or fear or anything else to intrude on our meal." He watched as her eyes shot to his and realized she had not been told often how beautiful she was. I need to rectify that, Lord, don't I? He didn't realize his heart had been caught already by Carrigan.

Chapter 6

Hearing the doorbell mid-morning on Saturday, Carrigan shook her head. It was becoming a very busy place, her home, she thought. How do I stop this? I need my solitude, Lord, and I'm not getting it. She peeked at the app on her phone and shook her head again. Cameron! Of course, it would Cameron. Who else would disturb her on a Saturday morning?

She reached to unlatch the screen door, standing back so he could enter, as she answered a call coming in. Bill was on the other end, asking her to head to a home on the edge of town. There had been a robbery that he didn't feel comfortable with. The agent had already talked to the homeowners, but they both felt something was off.

Carrigan headed for her office, Cameron staring after her, his mouth open to question her as she returned.

"I have to head out, Cameron. Bill just called."

"Let me go with you. Please? I don't feel good about you heading out on your own."

"I don't need a babysitter, Cameron. I have a job to do and need to get there." She saw the hurt look flicker across his face. "I'm sorry. That was not called for. Sure. Come with me, I guess. You'll have to stay outside though, you do know that?" At his nod, she almost shoved him out the door and locked up, heading for her vehicle.

Cameron ran to catch up with her, reaching to open her door, shrugging when she frowned at him before she slid behind the wheel. Shutting her door, he almost ran around the vehicle, afraid she really would take off without him.

Once more he sat, watching through the open window on his door as she worked through the investigation, talking to the homeowners, the responding officer, and some neighbours before she finally headed his way again, locking her camera and notes into the boxes in the hatch of her vehicle. She sat behind the wheel, her eyes on the house, a frown in place before she shook her head and turned to him.

"This hasn't been much fun for you. You had wanted to talk, I think?"

He nodded. "I did and don't even think of apologizing. You had a job to do and have done it well, I can tell." He shifted in his seat to watch her profile. "It's getting near lunch. How about we grab some sandwiches and head for the park? We can talk as we eat."

She nodded, heading for the snack bar near the park, thinking that was where he wanted her to go. A hand on her arm stopped her and had her pulling to the curb before turning to him.

"Not the snack bar, if that's where you're heading. Stop at my Aunt's and I'll run in and grab something for us. Do you have any preferences?"

He was back in short while and nodded as she pointed towards the park. They walked for a while before finding a table to sit at. She stared down at her sandwich, her thoughts muddled, not quite sure what was going on. She didn't remember anyone, any male she corrected herself, other than her father, who had put her first like that. The few dates she had been on had not gone well. That had turned her off dating. She jumped as his hands reached for hers and she heard his prayer. I need to stop jumping like this, Lord, only I have no idea how to stop it.

Cameron waited, watching closely as a shuttered look came over her face. How do I reach her, to see the real person under that mask?

"You wanted to talk, Cameron. What about?" Carrigan brushed off her hands after she had wrapped her lunch debris into a small package.

"I did, and now, I'm not sure how to start."

"At the beginning is usually the best place."

His head shot up and he gaped at her for a moment before a grin crossed his face. She sat there, a smirk on her face, mischief in the depth of her eyes. He was fascinated with the colour of them, not having seen green eyes quite like hers. He felt as if he could get lost in them and never find his way back home. A sudden thought flashed through his mind, that maybe, just maybe, he really didn't want to find his way home again, that with Carrigan he was home.

"I did. It's about that candlestick you found. Corbin thought it might be a game piece, but I don't think it was. It looks more the size of what you'd find in a dollhouse."

She stared at him before her eyes slid closed. "That's what has been bothering me.

My initial reaction was the same as Corbin but that never felt right. What you said does. But how does the thimble fit in?"

He shrugged. "Unless it's because you have to sew curtains and rugs and whatever for a dollhouse. You can't just go out and buy them."

"Actually, you can." She pulled out her phone at its incessant chiming. "It's my Mom." She looked frightened. "They never call me like this."

"Answer it." He reached to clasp her hand as she did just that.

"Mom? Something's wrong, isn't it? Are you and Dad okay?"

"We are, Carrigan. It's just that there's been a break in here."

"A break in? How did they get in? You have a really good security system."

"We do at that." Her father's voice rang across the line. "The wires were cut and the culprit was in and out very quickly, before anyone could respond."

She shot a look at Cameron. "What did they take, Dad? Mom? What aren't you telling me?"

"Your dollhouse. The furnishings for it. That's all they took. The police officer can't explain why just that."

"When did this happen, Dad?"

"Monday, we think. We were away for a couple of days and didn't get word until today when we got home. For some reason, the alarm didn't send to our cell phones like they should have."

"Dad, Mom. Please be very careful. I have no idea who did this, but it might tie into an investigation I'm involved in. Call Mark. Tell him. He's heading this way at some point and he needs to know this before he gets here."

"We will. Carrigan, when can we meet?"

"I'm not sure, Mom. Right now it's not safe. I'll explain when I see you, but I just know it's not safe to meet. Love you." She had heard the longing and love in her mother's voice, and as always, it broke her heart. She just couldn't go near them, she thought.

She pocketed her phone, cutting off the protests from her parents. Cameron watched her face, seeing the distress, fear and something else in it.

"Carrigan?"

She shook her head, bringing herself back to where she sat. Her eyes trained to the distance, she paused, not quite sure on how to proceed.

"What did they take from your parents?" He moved to sit beside her, an arm coming around her, knowing she needed that contact.

"My dollhouse. That's all they took, the dollhouse. The furnishings for it. Why?" She turned tortured eyes to him.

"Your dollhouse?" He stared at her for a moment before he looked down. This was strange, he thought. Why her dollhouse? "Do they know who broke in?"

She shook her head. "My parents were away and didn't find out until they came home early this morning. The thing is, their security system was disabled, just like yours." She watched as comprehension dawned.

"Just like mine? But why? I didn't know you before Wednesday. At least, I didn't remember you."

She nodded. "I know. But I think it has something to do with what you do. Cameron, you need to be very careful. This is far from over."

He shook his head. "I make jewelry boxes and small wooden caskets. The odd time I've made a scale model, just for friends. Nothing that would warrant something like this. I don't do dollhouses."

She nodded. "I know. This just doesn't make sense." She thought of the packet that she had received that morning. "The thing is, Cameron, I got another packet this morning. I haven't opened it yet, leaving it. I'm scared to."

He prayed for her, prayed as he had never prayed for anyone before. Then, he reached for her hand, gathering their garbage with the other one. At her car, he reached for the keys.

"Let me drive, please. You're shaken."

She searched his face, seeing the caring and compassion there, and nodded, sliding into the passenger's seat. Her hands clenched together, she thought back over her parents' words. Who, Lord? Who did this?

"Let's head back to your place. I want to be there when you open that packet." He shot her a glance when she refused to speak. "Carrigan?"

She shook her head to clear her thoughts. "I heard you, Cameron. I just don't know if that's such a good idea."

"It is. You can't do this on your own. Not any more." He pulled into her driveway, reaching to still her movements. "Let me get your door."

He handed her the keys and watched as she unlocked her home, disarming the security system. He studied it. It was a different one than he had. "Who set up your parents' security system?" When she named the company, his eyes shot to her. "That's the same company as mine. Chances are someone has hacked into their system and went after ours."

She reached for the packet, his hands on hers stilling her movement.

"Do you have any idea what would be in this?" When she looked up at him, he continued. "Let me call Tim. He's not on duty, but he'll come by. He promised me he would, that he would help us in any way he could. That's the kind of friend he is."

Tim watched as Carrigan opened the packet, hearing her cry of dismay as she stared down at it before her eyes raised to Cameron and then him. "This is from my doll house. I know it is."

Cameron wrapped her in his arms even as he watched Tim pull on gloves and pick up the object from the packet. "What is that?"

"A tiny tea cup, by the looks of it. You are absolutely sure it's from your doll house, Carrigan?"

She nodded. "It was specially made for me by a friend of my Mom's who did pottery. That friend died a couple of years ago from cancer, but she was adamant she had only made the one set. I have no reason to doubt her." She paused, a thought crossing her mind. "Check the bottom. You'll find my initials in tiny writing."

Tim squinted, then nodded. "They're there. Did you say your parents had a break in as well and all they took was your doll house and the furnishings? That is really bizarre."

"It is, but it isn't." The two men stared at her, as she pulled out her phone. "I need to put you in touch with someone, Tim, someone who can explain much better than I can." She sighed as she heard the doorbell ring. "What is going on?"

Tim headed for the door, opening to find an older man standing on the porch, back to the door, scanning the area around the house before he turned back.

“I’m sorry? I was looking for Carrigan.”

Carrigan appeared behind Tim. “Mark? Come in. You’re just the person I need to talk to.”

Tim and Cameron shared a look as Carrigan reached to hug Mark before she pulled him to the kitchen.

Chapter 7

Mark Hall studied the younger woman before him, seeing the stress in her that he hadn't seen six months ago when he had talked to her in person. He mentally shook his head. What was going on here?

"I talked to your parents. Your father called."

"I told them to. They told you what was taken?"

"They did. This doesn't make sense, Carrigan. Why your doll house and its furnishings?"

She pointed to the table. "That doesn't make sense either. It's one of mine."

He shot her a look before bending over to study the tiny cup. "What kind of games are they playing with you?" He straightened up, a stern look coming over his face.

She nodded. "Mark, I have no idea what it is all about. All I know is, is that I don't like it." She pointed to Tim. "He's an officer here on the force. And this is Cameron Steele. I talked to you about him."

Cameron finally understood that Mark was the officer she was expecting. He was just not what Cameron had expected.

A discussion ensued as to what the cup meant, but no clear decisions were made. Mark finally took his leave, promising to be back in touch with Carrigan in the next day or so. Tim headed off for the department, the tiny cup in an evidence bag.

Carrigan turned back from locking the door behind Tim, wrapping her arms around herself as she paced the living room. Cameron stood, a shoulder against the door jamb, waiting for her to speak. Finally, he spoke.

"Carrigan, what now? What do you do?"

She shrugged. "I have no idea, Cameron. I have no idea how far these men will go, if it is even the bank robbers. We can't prove it's them. And we can't prove it's not." She spun. "Now you see why I asked you to leave and not have anything to do with me."

"Unfortunately, my leaving won't made a whit of difference. They've connected us for some reason, and that reason is something I want to find out about." He pulled out his phone. "I'm calling Corbin."

She reached to stop him, her eyes on his face, even as she shook her head. "I think's he's already investigating something about that, and if you call him, he'll dig deeper. That could get him killed."

"You're serious about that, aren't you?"

"I am." She withdrew her hand from his arm. "I was there when the bank was robbed. I was shot at. I don't want to see anyone hurt. That includes your family."

He nodded. "I get that. But in the same instance, we don't want you hurt."

She backed away from him. "Please, Cameron. I am not sure what you're meaning, but I need time to absorb what is going on. Grant me that, please?"

He finally nodded. "Call me, Carrigan, when you decide. I don't want to lose touch with you."

Carrigan nodded. "I will, Cameron. Just a couple of days. That's all I'm asking."

She stood for a moment after hearing the door close behind him before she ran to lock it up. She was scared, frightened, no, struck with terror, she thought. They had found her parents, had found her, had connected her to Cameron and why that was, no one was sure.

She finally headed for her office and pulled out the files of the robberies she had been investigating, tracing her finger through the spreadsheet she had prepared. She nodded. It had to be them. She knew that for a fact, but just had to prove it. She shot a glance at her computer, then shook her head. No, she wasn't ready yet to talk to Mark. He had the information she had, but hadn't said if he had made the same connections that she had.

She turned to stare at the door, knowing at some point she did have to talk to Cameron again. She just needed to head him off for a day or so, until she felt safe enough to venture from her home.

Anger began to grow within her once more. This was not the first time she had felt like a prisoner in her home, or in her town. She wanted this to end. Lord, how do I do just that? How do I stop these people?

She dug back into her notes and observations, finally sitting back. She had the names now, she knew. That Mark would not be happy about, she knew. What did she do with the information now? She could pass it on to Corbin, but that would place him in danger, and she just couldn't do that to him.

She searched for her phone, finding it in the kitchen, and scrolled through her missed calls. Bill had call, leaving voice mail. She listened to it and then shrugged. He didn't need her on an investigation, he said. He just wanted to make sure she was fine. She sent a quick text back to him, not wanting to talk to anyone.

She searched further through her calls, seeing some from an unlisted number and some from a blocked number. Chills ran through her. They had found her phone number, now hadn't they? How did she protect herself if that was the case?

She reached for her keys, suddenly needing to be around people, and that was not like her. When she was frightened, she hid. Not this time, she thought. Now why would that be?

She slid into a booth at Angela's restaurant, reaching for a menu, but knowing she wasn't that hungry. Angela watched for a moment, then reached for the phone.

"Carrigan? What can I get you today?"

Carrigan jumped and then smiled up at Angela. "Sorry. I'm not really that hungry.

Maybe just some water and a ham and cheese sandwich."

"That I can get you. Are you okay?" Angela was concerned about Cameron's friend.

Carrigan shrugged. "As well as I can be, I suspect. Thank you, Angela."

Cameron hesitated as he walked into the restaurant, summoned by his aunt. He knew Carrigan had asked him to stay away from her, but when his aunt had called, he had to come. Something compelled him to.

He slid onto the bench across from her, her eyes on him as he did so.

"This isn't a couple of days, Cameron." She was trying hard not to smile at his grin.

"I know. Aunt Angela called, asking me if I knew you were here on your own. She's concerned about you."

"She should be more concerned about you." Carrigan accepted her meal with a quiet word of thanks. "You're not eating?"

"They'll know what to bring me." He grinned again, even as he reached for her hands, his head bowing as he said a prayer over their food.

Looking up at her, he commented, "You've discovered something."

She nodded, chewing on her mouthful of food before she swallowed it. "I have at that, and I'm not sure where to go with it. And before you ask, I will not go to Corbin."

"Then, let me help. If I can, that is. I'm concerned about a friend, Carrigan." He watched closely as she finally nodded. "This is not like you, is it?"

She stared at him. Most people never learned how to read her, but he had with just a few days and a few conversations. "How did you know?"

He shrugged. "I don't know. It's the truth, isn't it?"

"It is. I usually hide from people." She sighed. "What has changed, Cameron? Or rather, who?"

He shrugged, looking up to thank his cousin for his plate of food. He drew in a deep breath, relishing the aroma of the beef stew. "This is good. You should have had this instead of that sandwich."

She stared at him, snapping her mouth shut finally. "I had what I wanted. That's why I ordered a sandwich. I am not that hungry."

He nodded this time, concentrating on his food, idle conversation between the two of them. He finally sat back, his eyes on her, waiting for her to speak.

"What changed, Cameron? You were just a client. Now, you're becoming a friend. Can I do that?" She stared at the crumbs on the table before a finger reached to move them around.

"I think we can. One day at a time, that's all we can do. Listen, tomorrow's Sunday. Come to church with me." He waited, holding his breath until she finally looked up, searched his face, studied the look in his eyes, and nodded. He drew a deep breath. That had been easier than he thought.

"Why, Cameron? I have to know. Most people run the other way when they find out I'm dangerous to know. And I am that. I have had friends hurt by these monsters."

"Because you need someone with you, someone in your corner. I want to get to know you better. Dad used to be good friends with your father, did you know that?"

She shook her head. "They've never talked much about here. I have no idea why. Do you?"

"Dad said they left when you were what, six, eight?" At her nod, he continued, "He doesn't say much but he did say yesterday that your father was offered employment that he felt he had to take. That it would mean benefits and an easier life for your mother. Dad did say your father struggled financially here for a while, what with being ill."

Carrigan nodded, her eyes seeking the window at the front, where she watched the pedestrians pass by. "He's still not all that well at times. He's taking early retirement, he told me. He would like to move back here, to his home town. Mom would like that, too."

"And what about you? Do you want that?"

She shrugged. "I guess. It's just hard when I know trouble is following me all over."

"Do you think your parents don't know that or that they even care? They want to be near you." Cameron dropped money on the table, then reached for her hand, pulling her to her feet. "Enough of this. We need to go have some fun." He headed for the door and down the street towards the park.

"We do, do we? And just what do you consider fun?" She stared at the carousel in the park. "This? This is your idea of fun?"

"Have you ridden it lately?" When she shook her head, he pulled her with him, seating her on one of the horses, and then standing beside her, an arm around her back.

"Where's yours, mister?" She frowned at him.

"I think I'll stand right here." He just grinned at her frown before she sighed.

Cameron watched as she enjoyed the ride, her eyes closing at times as she felt the breeze on her face. Once the ride was finished, he helped her off and then pulled her with him, walking through the amusement park the town had set up to draw in tourists.

"This is new, isn't it?"

"It is. Our town was slowly dying, until someone willed the money to build this park. It draws people from all over."

She frowned, something niggling at her mind, but she shrugged it away. "That has made a difference, has it?"

He nodded. "It has. Now, where to?"

"I need to go home. I have some calls to make and for that I need my information at home. And no, you can't come with me."

He stood and watched her drive away from him, a shudder of fear coursing through him. Something was off. He spun in a circle, keys tight in his hand, not seeing anyone but knowing someone had been watching

Carrigan and now himself. Lord, we need
Your protection like we never have before.

Chapter 8

Cameron looked up from his work a week or so later, hearing his name called. His uncle stood there.

"Uncle Bill? To what do I owe the pleasure?"

Bill shook Cameron's hand and then wandered through the shop, studying the boxes and chests Cameron had crafted. "You are good, Cameron. You do know that?"

Cameron shrugged, feeling the pleasure that his uncle's praise brought to him. "I guess. But that's not why you're here."

"No, it's not. I've gone over all the paperwork on the incident here, talked to Tim, quizzed Carrigan until she's ready to smack me, I think. She's been right all along. Whoever it was did come in the door, not the window. But what did they want?"

Cameron shrugged. "As far as I can tell, nothing was taken. And that surprises me."

"As I am. Your tools would be worth a lot if someone tried to sell them. But what did they want?"

Cameron shook his head. "I'm at a loss, Uncle Bill. I asked Carrigan if she had any thoughts, and she just looked at me, and didn't say a word."

Bill nodded. "That's what I got from her as well. She seems to have some thoughts about it that she's not sharing." He sighed. "Have you talked with her today? She was to be in the office, and I haven't seen her or heard from her."

Cameron shook his head, squinting as he looked at the large clock on his wall. "No, actually I haven't. We're to meet for a meal in about thirty minutes. Do you want me to have her call you?"

"No, that's not necessary. Just send me a text that everything's okay with her."

Cameron watched his uncle walk away, and then turned back to his work, finally setting his tools away and walking over to the door, engaging the security system and locking the door behind him. He was worried now, and couldn't wait any longer to go find Carrigan. She was becoming important to him.

Carrigan looked up from her notes as she heard the doorbell, her eyes catching the time. Oh no, she thought. Cameron! She ran for the door, catching sight of him standing there.

"I'm sorry. I'm sorry. I meant to be ready. Come in, Cameron." Her words stuttered and stammered as she tried to apologize.

He swept her into his arms and hugged her tight even as she continued to try to apologize. He finally leaned back, shaking his head.

"It's okay, Carrigan. We have no time frame for tonight. Will you stop?" He finally convinced her that everything was fine, but she still apologized. That was until he reached down and kissed her, stopping her words.

She stilled, and then looked up at him as he leaned back once more, a frown on her face. "Cameron?"

"I had to. You wouldn't stop apologizing. It's the only thing I could think of to stop you."

She still frowned at him, her eyes studying his dark ones, before she moved back, his arms falling away from her, uncertainty in her movements.

"Carrigan, I apologize. I shouldn't have done that."

"Don't apologize, please, Cameron." She stood for a moment, then spun heading for the office. "Come here for a moment. I have something to ask you and something to show you."

Cameron stared up at the ceiling for a moment, knowing he had just blown whatever friendship they had going, before he followed her.

"What is it, Carrigan?"

"This." She shoved a paper into his hand. "I've been comparing the robberies I know about and ones that may be by the same gang. They've changed. They're not robbing banks just for money. They're going for safety deposit boxes. Coins. That's what they're taking now."

"Coins? Why?" Cameron was puzzled, that she could see.

"Because there is a black market out there for coins and collectibles. They can sell them all over the world and ship them out in anything and no one would ever know." She spun. "How difficult would that be?"

He shrugged. "I have no idea, not having ever done this." He looked down at her list, tracing the dates and towns with his finger. "They're moving closer to here, aren't they?"

"They are. I have Mark looking into that and at any break-ins like yours."

"What do you mean? Nothing was taken. It was just vandalism, at least, that's what Uncle Bill has said."

"There's always been something off about that, Cameron. Why break in and just damage paint and stain and some wood? Why not take your tools and sell them? Why not damage your finished products?"

He shrugged, not seeing where she was going with this. "I'm not following the reasoning, Carrigan. What are you trying to say?"

She leaned over his arm, pointing to various lines. "These. They are break-ins at business that have the potential to export products. Have you ever exported any of yours?"

He froze, his eyes on first the paper, then on the face so close to him. "A couple of times. I have an export license, yes. Are you saying they would use a legitimate business to export their stolen items?"

She nodded. "That's exactly what I'm thinking. Your jewelry boxes would be ideal, wouldn't they?"

He nodded. "They could be, but I don't see it happening. We're too far away from any port that would be used."

She sighed, as she took the papers back and tucked them away. "I pray you're right, Cameron, but there is still something I can't figure out." She picked up her phone, realizing she had muted it earlier. "Oh, my, your uncle's been trying to reach me."

"I know. He dropped by to see if I had heard from you." He grinned as she stared at him, mouth open. "Word has gotten around somehow that we were out together the other night."

She froze again, knowing that would be the truth. "We can't do this, Cameron. You will be at risk."

Cameron just swept her back into his arms, tightening his hold as she struggled to escape, waiting until she finally relaxed, her head down on his shoulder. "That's my decision to make, Carrigan. You can't go through this alone. You won't. Not any more. Mark is too far away to be of help to you. I'm here. Let me stay in your life, at least until this is over."

She finally nodded, her hair brushing his chin. "Just for now, Cameron. But you need to stay safe. I can't have you hurt. I couldn't live with that."

"Well, thank you, I guess." He grinned down at her as she frowned at him. "Stop frowning. You'll get wrinkles. At least that's what my Mom would say. Now, where to for dinner?"

She smacked him lightly before pushing away. "You were wanting to go out to eat? I have a grill and some meat in the fridge I was planning to cook. If you want to eat here, that's fine with me."

"That's sounds like a good plan." He reached for her, pulling her into another hug, one that she returned this time. "I'm just so afraid for you, Carrigan. I don't want to lose you, now that I've found you."

She leaned back to look up at him, a common position, she thought to herself, seeing he was so tall. "Thank you, Cameron. Anyone else I've dated have run after a couple of dates. They haven't been able to handle the danger that comes with me."

"And what danger would that be?" His eyes were serious as he studied her face, a face he was beginning to see in his dreams. "Dangerous to my heart? Because you are.

I'll give you fair warning. Once this is over, we will talk and talk seriously. I can't see a future without you in it. How's that for serious?" He tapped her chin to close her mouth.

"Cameron? No, I can't do this right now." She pushed at him, but he refused to let her go. "Cameron? Please? What do you want me to say? That when this is over, I won't run? That I'll stay here in Hope? Because I can't promise that. Only God knows His plans for us."

"I know that, love. We'll leave this discussion for another day, but I just wanted to serve notice that you're not walking away from me and I'm not walking away from you." He released her and turned to the back door, heading for the deck and her grill.

She watched as he left, her heart finally starting to calm down, but with a wonder in her eyes. Lord, I have no idea what's happening here but You do. Please, dear Lord, don't let another man break my heart. I can't handle that.

She turned, heading for her bedroom. She needed a few minutes. She listened to the sounds of Cameron in her kitchen, the fridge and cupboard doors opening and closing and felt content for the first time in years.

Cameron reached for his phone, his eyes on the back door. He could see Carrigan moving around inside. Corbin was on the line, asking when they could meet. He had information he wanted to give to both Cameron and Carrigan. Cameron finally agreed on the next night, provided Carrigan was free. He thoughtfully dropped his phone back into his pocket, his eyes on the grill as he flipped the chicken he had found in the fridge, knowing that this was where he wanted to be for the rest of his life, but knowing also that only God would lead that way.

They hadn't managed to meet with Corbin after all as planned. Mark had appeared, whisked Carrigan away, and told Cameron he wasn't sure how long she would be gone. The prosecuting attorneys needed to talk to her and in person was the only way they would do that.

Cameron had watched the vehicle leave, his heart falling. Please, come back to me, Carrigan. Don't leave me for good. He turned to his work to fill his time, the orders coming in fast and furious. He finally sat back on the Friday night, knowing he would need to work the next day, and not wanting to do that. His business was growing and he had to make decisions as to where it would go.

He finally reached for his phone, searching for a message from Carrigan and not seeing one. She had sent one that morning, saying she should be home in a few days, but that depended on the courts. He had talked to her the night before, hearing the fatigue in her beloved voice, and wanting to make it better for her. Only he couldn't. No one could. She had a path she had to follow.

He locked up his shop, heading for his truck, stopping in his tracks as he saw a form standing by the driver's door. A frown appeared on his face and then cleared away as he recognized the person.

"Carrigan? What are you doing here?"

She spun, hand to her throat, before she flew at him and into his arms. "Cameron. I'm so glad to be home."

He just stood, Carrigan locked in his arms, his head down on hers, for long how he was never sure. He finally set her back from him, his eyes tracing her beloved face.

"You're done?"

"I am. I had to testify after all, but they've managed to keep that to a minimum. That part is over." She walked back into his arms, holding on to him. "That's over, but it's not over, if you know what I mean? There is still someone out there, that wants to harm me."

"And Mark has no idea where they are?" He felt her head shaking. "But he's looking, right? He'll find them soon."

"He hopes to but he can't guarantee that he will. They've managed to cover their tracks well." She pulled back. "Now, what are we to do?"

"First, dinner I think. Are you up to going out?"

"Can we get some take-out and go to the park? I need fresh air. I've had to stay inside too long this week."

He tucked her into the truck, heading for his aunt's, knowing he would get a meal there, and then to the park, walking hand in hand with Carrigan until they reached the table they preferred.

He sat beside her, reaching for hand to say the blessing before they dug into their meal. He watched as she picked at her food, finally shoving it away only half eaten. He sighed to himself. This court case had taken a lot from her, he thought, as he wrapped an arm around her and pulled her to him.

"What now, Carrigan? Are you still planning on leaving town?"

"No, I don't think so. At least, that's not what I plan. I have no idea where God will lead. So far, He's been silent when I ask where I move to next."

"Then, I would say He wants you here, in Hope, for whatever time He says. I would like to see you stay here forever." He stopped, as her eyes searched his.

"Thank you, Cameron, for not pushing." She leaned her head against him. "You make me feel safe and beautiful and special. I haven't had that in years. But we do need to meet at some point with Corbin."

"We do, but not this weekend." He groaned. "I should be working tomorrow, you know."

"You've gotten that busy? What can I do to help you?"

It was his turn to search her face. "I could use help with the invoicing and packaging. That would leave me free to work on the boxes themselves."

"Then, that's what I'll do." She yawned and apologized. "I'm sorry. I've had little sleep for the last week."

"Let's get you home then, sweetheart. I'll pick you up around 8 in the morning, if that works."

Neither of them saw the man who walked by, intent on their conversation. He approached a man at the end of the walk who nodded and walked towards them, following as they headed for Cameron's truck.

Carrigan watched the next morning as Cameron lost himself in his work, her head shaking at his concentration. He had set her up on his computer, showed her his accounting program and the orders, and then left her to work on her own. She studied him once more and then was lost in her own work, finally rising to retrieve the invoices and the mailing labels. She searched for the correct boxes, reaching for the packing material. By lunch, she had his orders ready to go, and had called his aunt about a food order. Angela was delighted, she was informed, to prepare something and would hand deliver it.

Carrigan's hand rested on Cameron's shoulder and brought him back to the present and his shop. He wrapped an arm around her waist, pulling her to him.

"How much more do you have to do before you're done?" He looked at her as she started to laugh.

"I'm done. And your aunt is on her way with an order of food for us."

Cameron shot a look at the clock. "It's that late already? Where did the time go?" He looked down at his work. "I've gotten a good start on some of these. The recent orders have been for more simple boxes, thankfully." He turned to look at the table behind him, seeing the neatly stacked packages. "They are ready to go?"

"They are. Postage on them and all."

"Wow! I might just have to hire you away from Uncle Bill."

She laughed as she moved away, a finger tracing one of the boxes he had been working on, following the intricate roses and leaves and vines. "That not likely will happen, Cameron." She turned to watch him. "You keep dropping hints."

"I do, I know, and I shouldn't. We need to have a serious talk, young lady." He grinned as she shook a finger at him, rising to greet his aunt and take the food from her.

He locked the door behind her as they headed for his truck. He had loaded the packages into the back of the cab, ready to head for the post office on Monday morning. Standing and staring at them, he finally just shook his head. She had accomplished so much in such a short span of time.

Neither saw the truck that pulled out from a driveway and followed them, too busy with their conversation. Laughter filled the cab of his truck as he teased her relentlessly. She gave back as good as she got from him, one of the few who could, he thought.

Monday morning, Carrigan stood in her office at the insurance company, staring down at the package that sat there. She had

had a few days without receiving one. She sighed and picked it up, heading to tell Bill she was heading for the police department. He took one look and informed Suzie, the receptionist, that he was off with Carrigan and didn't know when either of them would be back.

Tim opened the package carefully, a frown on his face as he stared into it and then at Carrigan, who shook, fear on her face.

"What is it this time, Tim?" When he didn't answer, she moved forward, staring down into the small box. "A toy horse? What on earth?" She reached for it, his hand stopping her.

"Do you recognize this?"

She nodded, fear rising in her. "It is mine. And no, I'm not mailing these to myself to garner attention and sympathy."

"We didn't think you were, but I know some will say that." Tim handed it off to a tech. "I don't we'll find anything on them, but we'll take a look."

She shook as she stood there, her hands clenched on the back of a chair, her eyes staring ahead of her, not seeing the men around her. She was at a loss. This was getting too bizarre, she thought. First a small object, working up to this? Where would it end? She jumped as Tim touched her arm, spinning to face him.

"I'm sorry, Carrigan. I just need to asked you a couple of questions."

"Talk to Mark, please. Tell him it hasn't stopped. I can't do this." She broke from Tim's light grip and ran from the room, Bill's voice calling to her as he ran after her. He stopped her as she reached the door, his hand directing her to one side, away from the questioning looks thrown their way.

"Carrigan, before you run, stop for a moment." He looked around, seeing a bench they could sit on, and drawing her down to that. "Tim's a good cop. He'll help you figure this out. And I hear Mark is too. Don't run. Don't do this to Cameron or yourself. You two need one another."

She shook, watching her hands shake, before she finally nodded. "It's what I've had to do, Bill. I had to move constantly those first few months. We thought I was safe here. But they've found my home. They've found my work. They've found Cameron. Where does it stop?"

"We understand that, Carrigan, more than you think we do. Corbin's been talking to us. He's researching something he won't talk about, but he did say it was dangerous."

"Please, tell him to stop. He'll only hurt himself if he keeps up. They will kill. They have killed before and have threatened others."

"They threatened you, didn't they? And Cameron?" At her nod, he leaned back on the bench, anger on his face for a moment. "We'll fight them, Carrigan, in any way we can to keep you two safe." He held up a hand as she went to protest. "I've seen how Cameron looks at you. He's found his one and only in you. He has not said a word. He doesn't have to. You, I can't read. You hide your emotions well. That's what makes you a good investigator. But don't be afraid to let Cameron see how you feel."

She finally looked up at him, her heart on her face. "He's not the only one." Her voice was barely above a whisper. "I don't want him hurt. That's why I need to leave."

She didn't hear the footsteps approaching her or the rustle of fabric as someone sat down beside her, her eyes intent on Bill's face. She jumped as she felt arms surround her, then surrendered to Cameron's hug. Bill nodded at his nephew and then rose, a hand to Cameron's shoulder before he walked away.

"Cameron? How?"

"Tim called. He was worried you'd leave without saying good bye to him." She shifted so she could see his face. "Really. That's what he told me."

She snorted in an unladylike manner. "That's his story. I wouldn't have. I just panicked before I remembered you had said I wasn't alone. Your uncle reinforced that." She leaned against him. "What do I do, Cameron?"

"Stay. Date me. Let us get to know one another. And then we go from there. Just don't run from me, please, ever?"

He rose eventually, her hand in his, and led her to his truck, heading for his uncle's office. He pulled to a stop, twisting in his seat to watch her. "Uncle Bill said you can stay here, work from home, or come help me."

"I need to work, Cameron. I can't expect your uncle to pay me for not working."

"That is not the issue here, sweetheart. He's willing to pay you wherever it is you end up today." He watched as she struggled with the decision, finally making it for her. He backed out and headed for his shop, her eyes on him as he did so.

"Cameron?"

"It's okay, Carrigan. If you don't want him to pay you, tell him that. But you won't win that argument. He'll just tell you to investigate something at the shop." He laughed as she shook her head at him. "That's the truth. It's exactly what he would tell you."

She walked through the shop, not stopping at any one particular spot, needing the time to decompress from her fright earlier. Lord, what now? How do I continue? She turned so she could watch Cameron, hard at work on an intricate design he had left to come and rescue her. She stopped in her tracks. No one had ever done that for her, other than her father. What does that mean? I think I know, but until he says what he means, I won't know.

She finally sat at his computer, finding a stack of invoices there, and set to work, her mind slipping easily to the task, and finding she enjoyed it. She was content, that afternoon, spending time doing something for the man she realized she was coming to love, not knowing that in a few days her whole world would be turned upside down and both their lives would be at risk.

Chapter 9

Cameron opened the door to his shop a week later and paused, feeling something off but not sure what. He searched his building, finally shaking his head. Nothing seemed out of place, but he had that feeling someone had been in the shop, had circumvented his alarm system again. He walked to the touch pad, and then looking around and shading the numbers, changed his code. He frowned. There was something off about the number pad, he thought. He reached for his phone, calling for a tech to come and replace it. He made the decision to go with the same company Carrigan had at home. That might make him feel better but he wasn't sure. His next call was to a locksmith friend, who promised to come out shortly and change all his locks.

He searched his building once more, then stood staring at the doors and windows. Tim was right. He needed to upgrade them. It wasn't that he couldn't afford it. He had just kept putting it off. His phone out again, he placed a call to a cousin who had a window and door company, who promised to be right there and what had taken him so long,

102

anyway? Cameron laughed at Douglas' teasing before he set his phone down, staring at it.

He wanted to call Carrigan, to make sure she was fine, but she had told him last night when they spoke she had to head to the other side of town that morning for an investigation. She wasn't happy about it, either, he could tell. He had no idea who she was to see but he prayed for safety for her.

By the end of the day, Douglas had set in the new windows and doors for him, pulling all his workmen from other jobs to do that. The alarm tech from the new company had willing come back to finish his portion of the task, shaking his head at Cameron as well.

He looked around once more, still feeling watched. He would need to get Tim out there and search. Maybe he would find something Cameron had missed.

Carrigan looked up from the garden she was cutting back and smiled, rising to walk into Cameron's hug, brushing at the dirt she left on his shirt.

"I didn't expect to see you tonight."

He studied her face, getting lost in her eyes once more. "I didn't get a lot done today. I finally replaced the doors and windows, the locks, the alarm system."

"You did? Good. I was going to talk to you about those again." She watched his eyes, seeing something there. "But you think there's something more."

"I do.   Tim's going to drop by tomorrow with a tech friend and search more thoroughly. I feel like I'm being watched all the time."

She stepped back, reaching for his hand. "Take me to your shop. Now. I have an idea."

He reluctantly did just that, flicking on the lights as she prowled around the building, searching the benches and then working her way up the wall.   She finally stopped, stepping back to stand beside him, her back turned to the spot she had just studied.

"There's at least one camera here, Cameron.   That's why you're feeling watched. Let Tim know that. I'm sure there are more than one."

He led her from the building, locking up behind her. "What are the chances there are cameras outside?"

"I would think there would be. Someone has gone to a lot of work to put these in place. They're after something big. That scares me, Cameron. What are they after?"

He nodded as he tucked her once more into his truck and then slid behind the wheel. "I know. That's what puzzles me. I don't have access to what they might want, whatever that might be."

She shuddered at the thought. "They're getting bolder, aren't they? When will they stop?"

She pulled out her phone as it chimed, indicating a text message. She read it through and then thoughtfully pocketed her phone again.

"Carrigan? Bad news?"

She shook her head. "No, not really. That was Mark. The robber was given the maximum sentence. But he says the man's friends have upped their threat against me. For some reason, they're after me. I didn't see them."

"If you didn't see them, then it has to do with him. What did he do in the gang?"

"That no one has been able to quite determine. He's refused to say, and no one is talking about them. It is like they are just words on paper, don't really exist."

"But they do exist. You saw them. The people in the banks have seen them. They just haven't seen their faces."

She nodded. "They do exist. And they're after me. And I have no idea who they might be. They could be anyone I meet on the street, and more than likely are."

He reached for her hand, his warm against her cold one. She gripped his tight, feeling like she was holding on to a lifeline.

"Where do we go from here, Cameron? Someone is watching you."

"I know. I don't like that. I also don't like the fact that they're looking for you. And they will find you. That's a given."

She nodded, unable to speak for the lump forming in her throat. She knew her time in Hope was short and she didn't like that. She had planned to stay for the rest of her life, making her hometown her home again. Now, she was being chased from it.

"I haven't had any parcels in the last few days. I hope they have decided to move on to someone else."

Cameron's head was shaking negatively before she even finished. "I don't think so. I think they're coming up with a new plan, and that scares me, Carrigan. Who knows what they will do next."

"That's what I'm afraid of, Cameron. What happens next? And how do we prepare for it?" She turned to watch the lights flicking by as he drove towards her home. "I just want to go on with my life and that's not happening. Not with this hanging over me."

"You and I both." Cameron pulled into her driveway, watching as she reached for her seatbelt, his hand staying hers. "I don't want this to stop us seeing one another. I would like to take you out more often, as often as you will let me." He watched as she stared out the side window before looking at him.

"I have to think about that, Cameron. I'm still a dangerous person to be around."

"And those cameras in my shop? That doesn't make me dangerous as well?" He could feel the anger rising in him and worked to tamp it back down. "Let's just agree we're dating and trust God to protect us."

"Is it really that easy? I've never had that sense of protection that you seem to have. God hasn't been that for me. If He had been, why do I have to be on the run from these men? I pray, Cameron, but I don't have that. I don't have what you have. Why not?"

Cameron sorted through his thoughts, praying he would choose the right words. "I can't answer that, Carrigan. Only God can do that. But I know that He wants you to have peace in this. I want to be able to help you, to protect you, but I can't overstep our friendship."

She searched his face, finding an answer on it she didn't expect to find. "Then, I guess I'll have to let you, won't I? I just don't want you to be hurt, Cameron. And that I fear is exactly what will happen."

"We'll take one day at a time. Now, about tomorrow? What time are you finished?"

Chapter 10

Days turned into a week, and then into another week. Nothing had changed but everything had changed with them. They spent time together, and called each other when they were apart. Carrigan had received no further packages, and that puzzled her. She had talked to both Mark and Tim, but neither one had an answer for her as to why that had happened.

Tim had searched Cameron's shop and found a number of cameras inside and outside. He was puzzled as to why they had been installed. Cameron could give no explanation as to why. As he had stated to Tim, his was not a highly competitive business. And he didn't ship anything that would be considered contraband. Each box that shipped he had gone over, finding nothing out of the ordinary.

Carrigan had begun to split her time between Bill's office and Cameron's shop, finding she enjoyed the time spent in office work at Cameron's more enjoyable than her own work.

Cameron finally forced the issue one night as they walked along what they had come to call their path in the park.

"Come work for me full time, Carrigan. I can use you in the shop."

She shook her head. "There isn't enough office work to keep me busy. You know that."

He grinned at her. "But I can teach you how to paint and stain. That would be a big help."

She stared at him. "You're serious, aren't you?" At his nod, she sighed, her hand tightening on his. "I don't know. That's something I never thought about. Can I think it over and pray about it?"

He nodded, then hugged her. "You can. Just don't take too long."

She shook her head at him. "I'll take as long as I need. This is a big decision, you know."

Bill watched the young couple, happy for his nephew that he had found someone but concerned about the mystery still surrounding Carrigan. He talked to them both but they had just looked at each other and shrugged, not knowing what to say.

Carrigan looked up from her desk a couple of days later as Bill stopped in her doorway at work, a package in his hand. She froze, her eyes shifting between his face and the package.

"Another one, Bill?"

"I have no idea, Carrigan. I found it on the reception desk. It's addressed to you, but has no return address."

She rose and peered at the package, taking it from him and then heading for the door. "I'm off to see if Tim is working today."

"He is. I saw him heading in earlier today." Bill hurried to catch up with her. "Not another one. I thought they were done."

"Apparently not. I have no idea what will be in this one. And I really don't want to know."

Tim looked up as she approached the front desk, his eyes intent on her face before they fell to the package she held. He reached for it, knowing she likely wouldn't want to see what was in it, but that she had to.

Tim carefully opened the package, staring down at the metal object.

"Tell me, Carrigan. Did you have a toy car in the doll house?" He looked up at her sigh.

She approached him, peering over his arm. "That I did. But it doesn't look like the one I had." She reached for it, his hand coming out to stop her.

"Let me, Carrigan." He pulled on gloves and then gently removed the small metal car. "This is bizarre. It has your initials on it but you say you don't recognize it?"

"No, I don't. I've never seen it before. What is going on? Who is doing this? What they keep sending is just too weird."

"This isn't yours?" He questioned her again. "Then, why send it to you? What message are they trying to convey?"

Bill had listened in silence. He finally spoke, not sure how to exactly word his comments. "I think if you put them all together, you'll find they are sending clues or hints or warnings."

"That I can agree with." Carrigan stood back once more, her arms folded, a frown on her face. "I don't get what it would be though."

Tim studied her face before his eyes raised to Bill, who shook his head. He sighed to himself. This is not going good, he thought. How do we solve something like this when we have no idea who or even why?

Carrigan had been studying the tiny car, a frown in place. "What kind of car is that?"

Bill leaned around her to look more closely. "I would say a limousine of some kind. The make isn't important. It's a luxury car. Or perhaps they're hinting you'll be taking a trip somewhere."

Head shaking, she stepped back, away from both Tim and Bill. "I'm not travelling. That's a given. Tim, let me know what you find out about that." She turned and ran from the building, heading for her office.

Bill found her immersed in her work thirty minutes later as he paused just outside her door, a worried look on his face. He and Tim had discussed what Tim could share, but neither of them had any idea who or what. Tim had mentioned he would be in touch with Mark. Maybe he would have an idea.

Carrigan knew Bill was outside her door but refused to look up. She had stuffed everything going on with her to the back of her mind, determined not to let it ruin anything of her life any more. If something came out of it, she would deal with it then.

Lord, she prayed, help me to solve this quickly. I feel like my life is on hold and I do not like that, not one bit. Please, Lord?

Carrigan's eyes turned to the pile of folders on her desk and frowned. She reached for them, sorting quickly through them and pulling out the ones she wanted. She spun, staring at her filing cabinet across and the room and was on her feet, once more sorting through files.

She paused as she stared at the stack. There was a lot of work to do, she thought, before she was out of her office and heading for the other investigators, who looked surprised at the questions she was asking, but nodding in agreement before they too searched through their files. Carrigan was sure she was on to something but until she had the facts in front of her, she wasn't certain.

It took a week to go through all the files and gather the information she needed. She finally sat back, staring at the spreadsheet she had prepared and printed. It had shocked her, saddened her, but really didn't surprise her. She rose, a copy of the paper in hand, and searched for Bill, finding him in the break room, staring at the pot of coffee as it perked.

"It won't drip any faster staring at it, you know." Carrigan smiled as Bill jumped and then looked around at her.

"You're so quiet, Carrigan, I didn't hear you." He poured his coffee and then one for her, ignoring the shaking of her head. "You need it. From the looks of it, we'll be in a meeting for the rest of the afternoon. Come on back to my office."

Bill sank thankfully down into his chair. It had been a long week for some reason, and he was glad it was Friday. He stared at Carrigan for a moment, before he spoke.

"What do you have there, Carrigan? I can already tell it's not good."

She shook her head as she handed over the papers. "It's not. I went back over a lot of the investigations for the past five years. I was shocked at how many small valuable items were stolen."

He gazed as her for a moment before his eyes dropped to the papers. There was silence in the office as he read, except for the soft sound of flowing water from the desktop fountain he had and the occasional shuffle of paper as he turned a page. The odd bits of conversation from outside his office drifted to them. Carrigan prayed that he would see where she was going with this without her having to explain. She wasn't even sure she could make a reasonable explanation.

Bill turned back to the first page and re-read the material. This girl is good, isn't she, Lord? He finally sat back in his chair, the chair creaking slightly as it moved, his finger tapping the papers he had laid on his desk. A thoughtful expression crossed his face before he looked up at Carrigan, who was watching his every facial expression, not sure even then if she had done the right thing or was even on the right track.

"You're good, Carrigan. The others have come to me over the last week, expressing their concerns about what you were digging up, but also telling me that you were relentless in finding out the facts, not just hearsay. That is what makes you the investigator you are. All of them have said they would never have connected the thefts if you hadn't. Terry talked to a friend in another town who's an investigator, and that friend is now searching through their files." He paused, his eyes dropping down to the papers, before he looked up at her again.

"Carrigan, this is dangerous. If they even suspect you are on to something, they'll come after you."

She shrugged. "They already are. I just didn't know why. Now, I think I know part of it. But what I don't get is why they're sending me those objects? Why steal only my dollhouse and its furnishings? That has made no sense." She looked down at her hands that she had clasped tightly together. "I'm still not sure where this will all lead, though. Bill, what have I done?"

"What do you mean? What have you done? Other than digging into this and finding a link, I don't think you've done anything."

She shook her head as she looked up at him, a distressed look in her eyes. "No. I have done something and that made them come after me. I'm not even sure anymore if it's related to the bank theft or not."

"I think it is. They needed money to continue what they're doing. As far as I can see, none of the stolen items have been recovered or pawned or sold on a black market. We would hear about that." He leaned forward, forearms resting on his desktop. "We need to talk to Tim and that Mark. Can you call him and arrange for him to come? I'll talk to Tim."

"What are you thinking, Bill?"

"I'm thinking that this is much bigger than we even can imagine. The break-in at Cameron's shop is part of it. That much I know. If they have amassed items to ship outside the area, then they will need some way of doing just that. What better way than to use a legitimate business?"

She gasped, then swallowed hard to drive down the lump that had gathered in her throat. What are they up to, she questioned? And just where do I fit in?

"Bill, can I ask a question?" At his nod, she swallowed hard again, not quite sure how to frame the question. "When you sent me to Cameron's that day, was I the only investigator available? Or did you have a special reason for that?" She waved her hand. "Forget that question. I don't think it's relevant."

"No, it is. Sam was here, but was tied up on a conference call. Josie was away that day on a personal leave day. Andy was in court. Terry was on vacation. That left you. I would have likely sent you anyway, as you didn't know Cameron as well as the others. They would have taken it seriously, but not to the extent you did. You saw something that they may have overlooked, knowing what he does. That candlestick. I can't figure out what it means, but you saw it and questioned if it belonged there.”

She nodded, her eyes thoughtful as she studied the older man’s face. “It was just so odd. I mean, it could have been part of his work, but it just didn’t fit with what I was seeing in the shop that day.” She watched him nod. “That’s what you’re talking about, isn’t it?”

It was Bill’s turn to smile at her. “Exactly that.” He rose, his hand reaching out to pull her to her feet. “Come on. Let’s go talk to Tim and see if he can help with what he has on these break-ins. And then you need to go find Cameron. He’s been putting in some long hours and needs a break. It’s Friday, isn’t it? Tell him to take you out for dinner. Here. Dinner’s on me.” He reached into his pocket and then tucked some bills into her hand, despite her protest. He just grinned at her as she headed for her office and another copy of her spreadsheet.

Tim looked up as the desk officer spoke to him before he peered around him to where Carrigan and Bill stood. He read correctly that Bill was angry but that Carrigan was unsure of herself at that point. He walked towards them, assessing them once more as he got closer to them. He nodded as Bill spoke rapidly, explaining what Carrigan had found, his eyes scanning the material, and then raising to Carrigan.

"What made you think of this, Carrigan? It doesn't follow that you would make the connection from Cameron's incident."

She shrugged. "God, I guess. I need this over, Tim, and it won't be over until you catch these people. I just pray no one else is hurt by them."

Chapter 11

Cameron looked up, a frown on his face, as he heard his shop door open and close, glancing at the clock as he did so. It was late. He had wanted to be finished earlier today. He set down the wood he had in his hand and walked towards the front, stopping for a moment, a softened look coming to his face as he saw Carrigan standing just inside the door. He walked towards her as she turned.

"Carrigan? I didn't expect to see you tonight." He reached to hug her, just holding her for a moment as he sensed the stress she was under. "What's wrong?"

She shrugged. "I need a lift, if you can give me one?" She leaned back, holding up her hand with the folded money in it. "Bill sent me to find you. He gave orders for you to take me out to dinner."

"He did, did he? Then I guess I must, mustn't I? Just be a couple of minutes." He turned to leave when she reached for his hand, pulling him back around.

"We need to talk, Cameron, as well. But first, let's set aside everything and just enjoy a meal."

Cameron stepped back for a moment, his eyes on her face, before he nodded. "Sure. Whatever. Where do you want to go?"

"Not to your aunt's. Not tonight. I can't handle going there." She paced, arms crossed around her abdomen, as she ignored the questioning looks being sent her way.

Cameron carefully shut down his equipment and set away the products he needed to. He stared down at his desk for a moment, knowing he needed to work, but glancing up at Carrigan, knew she needed him more than the paperwork did.

He locked the door behind them, his hand coming up to cradle her elbow as he led her to his truck.

"Where do you want to eat?" His eyes searched her face, concern on his as she refused to look at him.

She shrugged. "I really don't care, Cameron." She stared out the window, waiting for him to start his truck and pull away. When he didn't, she spoke. "What are you waiting for?"

"For you, I guess. I'm not sure what's going on, Carrigan, but something is."

She finally nodded. "There is, Cameron, but I just don't know what it is or how far it reaches." She finally turned to him. "And I'm afraid for you. They've targeted your business and I think it's to use it to ship out contraband. That will get you in trouble and maybe even jail. I don't want that to happen to you or your family."

"Carrigan, you can't make that kind of decision for me." He was getting frustrated and knew it, tamping down his rising anger at the men responsible for the thefts. "What did you go and do?"

"Nothing. I just researched some stuff, talked to your uncle, to Tim, to Mark, to the other investigators. Right now, we're not sure where we stand or where we're going with this."

"Don't do it!" His voice was harsh with unspoken feeling.

She stared at him, defiance in her look. "Don't tell me what to do, Cameron. This has affected my life for so many years, I can't even begin to tell you how much I want this over." She shook off the hand he laid on her arm. "I think you need to take me home, please."

"Don't, Carrigan. Please!" He stared through the windshield, not seeing the sun as it was setting, sending out the pink and orange and red rays over the land. "I don't want you hurt. I don't want to lose you."

"You don't want to lose me? Really? Just what does that mean?" She shoved open her door and ran from the truck, heading for the street, not heeding his call as he ran after her, catching her into his arms, holding tight as she struggled against him.

"Let me go, Cameron! You have no right!" She shoved at arms that refused to loosen, her body twisting and turning in her efforts to get away, her hair lashing at his face.

"Carrigan! Stop! Please! You said you wanted to talk. Then, let's talk!" He finally got through to her and she stilled, her body tense in his arms. His forehead on her shoulder, he breathed hard, trying to catch his breath before he spoke. "No, I don't want you hurt or, even worse, dead. And that is a very real possibility. Please! Come with me. Let's get something and go to our bench in the park."

He waited as she stood, not knowing if his words had reached her or if she really was done with their friendship. Lord, not that. I can't stand to lose her. She's become so much a part of my life and my heart. Please, Lord?

She finally shoved at his arms, making him drop them from around her, and walked a few feet away from him, staring into the gathering dusk before she spun around and stomped back towards him.

"You can't control what I do, Cameron. We're just friends, right? You can give your opinions and I can take them but ultimately I have to make my own decisions." She searched his face, her next words dying on her lips, as she saw something there. "Cameron?"

"Carrigan. Just listen, okay? You wanted to talk. You didn't say about what, but I gather it's about what you've been up to the last week or so. You've been distracted and distant." He held up a hand at her protest. "You have been. And I get that. But I thought we were friends. Friends don't shut one another out. And how much time have you actually spent in prayer about this?" She was silent, her eyes watchful, waiting for him to continue.

When he didn't, she finally spoke. "Cameron? Just where are you going with this? And yes, I have been praying harder over this than anything else. I have had to. God is the only one who can lead to the conclusion of this and that's what I want. This has consumed so much, too much, of my life and I want it over."

"I'm sure you do. Just don't shut me out, please? That's all I ask." He crossed the few feet between them, his hands reaching to cup her face. "You've become too important to me for me to stand by anymore. Let me help you. You've said they're after me. Let me help catch them."

She finally nodded and leaned into his hands. "So, is dinner still on the table or have we gone too far past the point where we can share a meal in peace?"

He laughed as he caught the grin she was trying to hide but also her vulnerability she was showing him. That he knew she didn't do to many people. He reached to hug her, her arms finally wrapping around him.

He spoke gently, his breath whispering against her ear, moving the strands of hair. "Do we still go out for a meal?"

She nodded. "I guess. But where?"

"Let's see how much Uncle Bill gave you and then we can plan." He stared at the bills she handed him. "He was serious, wasn't he? This calls for a dress-up dinner."

She stared at him. "A dress-up dinner? Do you realize how late it is already?"

He nodded. "I do. So how be we put this off until tomorrow? You're exhausted, I can tell. Let me take you to your home, go home myself and find somewhere we can spend Uncle Bill's money tomorrow."

She shook her head, a distressed look on her face. "That's not what he said. He was specific as to going out to dinner tonight."

"He won't care, Carrigan. He'll be fine with us going out tomorrow. I know he will." He pulled out his phone, scrolling through his contacts to find his uncle's number, when her hand stopped him, her fingers closing over his.

"No, it's okay, Cameron. It's just everything has built up so much this week and I'm not thinking straight."

He studied her for a moment, before he grasped her hand and pulled her back to his truck. "In you go. We'll find something to eat tonight, using some of his money then, and tomorrow we'll spend together. That is, if you want to."

He slid behind the wheel, still waiting for her answer. He watched her profile, seeing the conflicting emotions on her face, and knowing that she had issues she was working through, that only God would be able to help do just that. He finally saw the moment she acquiesced, a tiny nod of her head, and a barely audible voice agreeing to his suggestion.

Lord, please help my friend. She's afraid of something or someone and I want to help her. Only I have no idea how to do just that. He finally pulled away from his shop, heading for a local cafe, not seeing the car that pulled out and followed him, parking where the occupants could watch them. The two men conversed, their conversation becoming heated, their hand gestures attracting the attention of passersby.

Chapter 12

Drawing to a stop in front of Carrigan's the next morning, Cameron shuddered, and not from cold. He felt the danger closing in and just couldn't believe it was happening to him. He didn't do things like this. He had never been in trouble. Not even when he was a teenager. His brother, Corbin, had been the one who skirted close to that, but Cameron had never done that.

He walked towards Carrigan's front door, a frown on his face. Her door was wide open and that was not her. He hesitated at the open door and then entered, calling out to her. He walked through her house, seeing her purse in her office, her keys on the kitchen counter, but no sign of her. He walked back out the front door and circled the house, checking every nook and cranny that he could find. She was not there.

He frowned once more before pulling out his phone and calling Tim, who he knew was on patrol that day. Tim was there in less than five minutes, responding from a break-in at a nearby property.

"Cameron? What's up?" Tim pocketed his sunglasses, his keen eyes taking in the concern radiating from his friend.

"Carrigan's missing. We had plans for today and now she's not here. She would have called if she hadn't been able to keep our date."

Tim nodded as he walked towards the house. "You went through it?"

"I did. Just to see if she was there. Her purse is there. Her keys. I even looked around outside."

Tim motioned for Cameron to stay outside as he too walked through the house.

"This is bizarre, Cameron. She wouldn't just take off like that."

"I know she wouldn't. So where is she?"

A voice from behind them had Cameron jumping and then spinning, his eyes on the woman standing there.

"Cameron? Tim? What's going on? I left that door closed when I went next door." Carrigan stood there, hands on her hips, a frown on her face, the sunlight filtering down on her hair.

"It was open when I got here. I looked for you and then called Tim." Cameron approached her. "Where were you?"

"I had to run next door for a moment. I took my extra key. Everything was locked up. I know it was." Carrigan moved to enter the house, stopping as Tim's arm blocked her way. "Tim? Why can't I go in?"

"Because if this is not the way you left it, someone else did. We need to go through it."

"It's my house, Tim. I will enter it." Carrigan moved forward, trying to bypass Tim and enter her home, only to have Cameron reach and draw her back. "Cameron! Let me go!"

"Not a chance, Carrigan. Tim is right. He needs to go back through your house, now that he knows you are safe. Let him do what he needs to. Carrigan! You are not going in there." Carrigan struggled to get away from Cameron, just like she had the previous night, and Cameron did what he needed to. He simply tightened his arms around her and lifted her off her feet and carried her back to his truck, setting her on her feet beside it.

Shooting him a dark look, Carrigan broke free and headed back for her house. Cameron watched and then reached for her, shoving her into his truck before he ran around and started it, pulling away before she could jump from it.

"Cameron! Just what are you doing? Take me back to my home. I need to be there." She just could not believe he had done what he had just done, left her house, not letting her go back to it.

"I can't, Carrigan, not if you are going to interfere in Tim's investigation. I thought better of you. You're an investigator. You know you can't be in there." Cameron was growing frustrated and knew he had to tamp it down, that she didn't deserve to be on the receiving end of it.

She glared at him before she turned away, to stare out the window. She finally sighed and turned back. "I'm sorry, Cameron. You're right. I can't be in there. Will you take me home now?"

He waited, not sure if she was really contrite or simply saying what he wanted to hear. His heart raised in prayer as he watched her, finally turning the truck and heading back to her home.

He left her sitting in his truck, with strict orders not to move, as he headed towards Tim. Corbin had appeared, his eyes following his brother before he stopped by the open truck door, leaning back against the truck.

"What? You're here to make sure I behave?" Carrigan's disgruntled voice had Corbin stifling his laughter, knowing she would not appreciate the humour he saw.

"Nope. Just happened to stop by. I was heading this way. We need to talk, Carrigan. I hear tell you've been doing some investigations. I would like to share what I know with you."

She shook her head. "I haven't really done much, Corbin. That's the truth." She stared towards her home, her heel kicking idly against the frame of the vehicle.

Corbin shook his head. "Are you serious? Of course you know something. That's why they're after you. What is it you know?"

She shrugged, finally looking at him. He drew a deep breath at the devastation and fear he saw lurking in her eyes before shooting a glance towards his brother. Cameron, you need to deal with this, not me. She's your lady, not mine.

Cameron paused for a moment as he headed back towards Carrigan, searching her face and then turning towards Corbin.

"Corbin? What are you doing here?" Cameron reached to pull Carrigan from the truck, wrapping an arm around her to hold her close to his side.

"Looking for Carrigan. We need to talk, Cameron, you, Carrigan, and myself. If we pool resources, we might be able to figure out what's going on before someone gets hurt."

Cameron was puzzled, not having had the talk with Carrigan he needed to have. "I don't understand what's going on, but Tim wants you to walk through your house, Carrigan, and see if anything is missing."

Carrigan pushed away from him, almost on a run to her house, leaving the brothers staring after her.

"Just what did you say to her?" Cameron rounded on Corbin, who stepped back, hands in the air.

"Just that we needed to talk, to try and figure out what was going on before your lady gets hurt." Corbin reached out a hand to his brother's arm, stopping his forward motion. "Listen, Cameron. Hit me if it makes you feel better. But she's been investigating the robberies over the last few years and has made some kind of a connection with them all. Uncle Bill was over last night at Mom and Dad's. He's worried about her."

Cameron stood, his eyes on the house, before he turned to Corbin. "Just what are you saying, Corbin?"

"That she's found out something and whoever this is will go after her even more. And it involves you now, as well."

Cameron nodded, fear rising within him, fear that he tried to tamp back down with a prayer and a wish. "I know. She told me that last night." He ran his hands through his hair. "I just don't know what to do any more, Corbin. I can't tell her to stop. She won't, even if Uncle Bill pulls her off the cases. She'd just quit and continue on her own."

"No, I won't quit. Get that straight, you two." Cameron looked up at her, seeing the hurt on her face. "I came back to get you to help me go through the house. Never mind, Cameron. Tim and I can do it on our own." She spun and ran for the house, not letting him see the tears she angrily brushed away, Tim's eyes on her face and then raised to where Cameron stood, before he moved to walk with Carrigan into the house.

"That went well. Thanks a lot, Corbin. Now I have to go make peace with her." Cameron moved away from his brother, not responding to Corbin's soft "I'm sorry". He appeared at Carrigan's side, not saying a word as she paced through the rooms.

"I don't see anything missing, Tim. That's strange." She looked down at her notes on her desk, searched her computer, and then dropped into her desk chair. "Nothing has been taken. So why break in?"

"A warning, I suspect, Carrigan." Tim pocketed his note book. "If you find anything, let me know."

Cameron stood in the office doorway, an unsettled feeling in his heart, knowing something was different. "Carrigan, what's different about this room? Something is."

She spun to stare at him, her mouth open before she snapped it closed. She rose, a dark look on her face, as she stalked towards him. "Don't tell me that. I don't want to hear something is different."

She paced the room, her eyes searching, before she stopped in front of the fireplace, her hands touching the ornaments on the mantle. She froze, a cry drawn from her that she had no control over.

Cameron was at her side before the cry died away, his arms around her. Tim stood there as well, his eyes shifting between Carrigan and the mantle.

"What is it?" Tim's voice was stern, even as Carrigan struggled to back away.

"That ornament. Yes, that one." Tim stared at the one she was pointing at. "That's my Mom's. She gave it to me for my doll house. It was her mother's, she said, but it fit just perfectly in the living room." She watched as with a gloved hand, Tim reached for the tiny spinning wheel.

"What is going on, Carrigan? What are they doing? Why keep sending you bits and pieces of stuff?" Tim studied the spinning wheel before carefully stuffing it into an evidence bag.

"I have no idea, Tim. I just want this over. I don't know why they keep doing this."

Cameron tightened his hold on her, fear growing stronger. He had no idea who it was that was targeting her, but someone was.

"Carrigan, how sure are you that this is related to the bank robbery?"

She shifted in his arms so she could see his face, her hand raising to rest against his cheek. "It has to be, Cameron, but I don't see how it is. Mom mentioned this morning that she had forgotten to tell me they came home about a year ago and found the house unlocked and the security system off. They thought maybe they had just forgotten to lock up after themselves.”

Tim froze, his eyes on the floor. “No, they didn’t.” He looked up, his eyes locking on Cameron’s, seeing the understanding there. “Whoever this is entered their house all those months ago for a reason. I think it was to check out your doll house. But why didn’t they take it then?” He gave a groan of frustration as his phone chimed and he pulled it out. “Sorry, guys. I have to run. There’s been another break-in. What is going on in this town? We have never had the number we’ve had in the last six months.”

“Wait, Tim. I noticed the increase in the number. But nothing is being taken in some of them. Nothing is changed, moved. Nothing.” Carrigan watched as Tim nodded, his eyes thoughtful as he in turn watched her. “What are they planning? There has to be something big coming up. Any VIPs coming through town? Any announcement of major funding for any projects? Any new developments?” She was throwing out suggestions, she knew, that might have nothing to do with the robberies and break-ins but she was getting desperate to get out from under the burden weighing her down.

Tim nodded, knowing just what she was up to. “I agree, Carrigan. Our detectives are seeking out just that, but so far, haven't made a connection. But then, we hadn't made the connection you made of all the break-ins and robberies over the last four or five years. I heard back from Mark. He's concerned that if that gets out, whoever is after you will escalate their attacks. And it's not just about you anymore, Carrigan." He nodded at Cameron, who had stood, silent, taking in their conversation even though he really didn't understand it all. Tim saw Corbin standing near the doorway, nodding in agreement with Carrigan. "You both need to stay safe. That means you stop investigating, Carrigan. I can't force you to, but if your investigation breaches ours or interferes with it, the chief will charge you. Make no mistake about that."

"I won't do that." Her voice was low enough the three men had to strain to hear it. "I just don't want to continue living like this, not free to travel, to see my parents, to do what normal people do." She spun in Cameron's arms, reaching to hug him, her face burrowing into his shoulder.

Tim's hand rested briefly on her shoulder, then tapped at Cameron's before he walked past, stopping for a word with Corbin, who nodded, his eyes on his brother, worry on his face.

Chapter 13

Caitlin tapped at Carrigan's door before it popped open suddenly, startling her. Corbin reached to pull her in, sticking his head out to search the area before he slammed the door closed and locked it.

"Corbin? Just what are you doing? Cloak and dagger stuff? Where's Cameron? I got his SOS and headed here." She headed for the voices in the kitchen, stopping for a moment to assess her brother before turning her eyes to Carrigan.

"Caitlin? Good you're here." Cameron rose to hug her, drawing her back to the table and a chair. "Sit. We're trying to brainstorm, but Carrigan and I are too close to the situation. Corbin's of no help to us. He's adding information that is confusing us."

Carrigan snorted. "Confusing you, you mean. It makes perfect sense to me."

Cameron just shook his head. "Nope. You're as confused as I am."

"And just how do you think I can help?" Caitlin grinned at Carrigan before frowning at her brother.

"Carrigan has connected all sorts of information. We just need to know if on any of the sites you may have been at you saw anything you thought odd or out of the ordinary."

"Cameron! You know I can't talk about our clients!"

"You can. I called your boss and he said given what's happening and what Carrigan could tell him, you could talk about what sites you found something odd on. I know you've been to some of these."

Caitlin shot her brother a dark look. "Next time, let me talk to my own boss. Stay out of that." Cameron just shook his head, not looking sorry at all. "What do you need, Carrigan?"

"Just your observations on these places. Mark the ones you had to go into and then let me know if you thought anything was off, odd, whatever." Carrigan moved away from the table, back to the counter where she had been working on a salad.

Corbin stood beside her, working in silence with her as he prepared the sandwiches she pointed to. He finally just stood, hands still, eyes on the window, a thought crossing his mind. He reached for a towel to wipe his hands and pulled out his phone, excusing himself to make a call. Something Caitlin has just muttered triggered a memory and he needed to research it while the idea nudging at the edge of his mind was fresh.

Cameron rose and walked after his brother, leaving the two ladies in the kitchen, quiet conversation between them.

Carrigan finally set the salad on the table and reached into the cupboard for plates.

"What have you come up with, Caitlin? I know you have. I recognize that look. I look the same way, I'm told." She grinned as Caitlin raised her head and frowned at her.

"I have, Carrigan, and I don't like it." She shot a glance towards the back door, knowing her brothers were outside on the deck. "I don't want to say anything in front of Corbin, but it looks as if his girlfriend's father might be involved in this. He has had four of his businesses hit as well as his office. No one has that much bad luck."

Carrigan slid into the chair beside her, reaching for her notes. "I saw that and wondered. You're right. Someone was after something there. What exactly does he do?"

Caitlin stilled, her eyes wide with first shock and then fear for her brother. "He's into imports and exports. Tiles, etc. That kind of stuff."

Carrigan nodded. "That is what I had determined. But is he involved in more than that? I have asked Mark to search with his resources rather than Tim. It would get out if someone here was looking."

"Looking into just what exactly, Carrigan?" Corbin's voice behind her had her sliding her eyes shut in frustration.

"We're looking into everyone who has had robberies or break-ins." She went to speak further, but Caitlin's hand on her arm drew her gaze to the other woman, who was shaking her head.

"I'm sorry, Corbin, but Eva's father's had four break-ins at his businesses and at least one at his home." Caitlin watched as her brother absorbed the news, even as Cameron finished off the sandwiches and set the plate on the table and then sat himself near Carrigan.

Corbin hunted for drinks for them, finding juice and water in the fridge, before he sat, then reached for his sister and brother's hands to say a blessing on their food. He ate mechanically for a while, quiet conversation going on around him before he finally spoke.

"Carrigan?" At her glance at him, he smiled. "It's okay. I've suspected something for a while. That's why Eva and I are no longer dating. Her father made her back away."

"You've been investigating and got too close?" Carrigan's quiet words startled the other two. They had not made that connection, not quite yet.

"I had been. That's why I wanted to talk to you today." He looked down, a dark look on his face. "I don't get it, though. He has money, more money than he can ever spend. He donates all over the place. But now I have to wonder if the money is from legitimate sources."

"Or the proceeds from crime." Cameron finished his brother's thought. He chewed absentmindedly on his sandwich before he swallowed and turned to Carrigan. "Carrigan? What can you tell us?"

She shook her head, before searching the faces around her, her eyes lingering longest on Cameron. "I don't have proof. Just speculation. That doesn't help."

"It will, if we can research it. I have friends who can look into things for me without it getting around town that I'm the one."

Cameron reached for the paperwork Carrigan was rolling into a tube and flattened it out, reading through it, before he reached for a pen and started making notes, asking quiet questions of his brother and sister, clarifying her intent with Carrigan. He finally sat back, shock on his face.

"This is crazy!" He looked up at Carrigan's snort. "What? You don't think it is?"

"I know it is. Cameron, that's what has me worried. Your business. They can use it for exporting and importing contraband. You might never know it." She froze, as her voice died away. "When you had your break-in, had you had any imports come in? Anything ready to export?"

He shook his head. "I haven't done anything like that in months. Not outside of the country. I have some that have gone across the country but that hadn't been in weeks." He looked back at her. "You think they broke in to plant something?"

She shrugged. "Maybe. Or just to check it out, to see if they could use your boxes." She rose, heading for her office, before she returned, setting pictures in front of him. "Look through these. Tell me what you see or don't see."

She waited as he leafed through the photos, a frown on his face as he set a number to one side. He finally looked up, his eyes on his brother's face.

"You suspected this, didn't you, Corbin?" At Corbin's nod, he sighed. "You are correct, Carrigan. I see things that were moved from where I left them. I thought it was the lab techs that had moved them, but I realize now they would not have moved a thing. Not unless they had to." His finger tapped the photos he had set to one side. "In every one of these, something is different from what I left the night before. Subtle changes but I know where I leave things. I have to."

Carrigan reached for the photos, knowing before she looked that he would have picked up on most of what she had. "These are the ones I wondered about, Cameron, but I didn't know you or your work habits at the time. I know now that's not how you leave your tools, your wood. But what I don't get is why dump out the paint and stain?"

"A threat." Corbin nodded as Cameron stared at him. "A threat, Cameron. A subtle one but coupled with the drone, that's exactly what that was. Cooperate with them or worse things would happen."

Cameron shook his head. "But no one has approached me. Not yet, anyway. I searched through my customers and had someone look into any I suspected. All have come back as legitimate."

Carrigan shook her head. "That's what you'll find, Cameron. They're not going to jump up and shout "look at me". They stay under the radar so you don't suspect anything. Mark is looking into some things for me. There are a couple of names I have seen on other reports. And no, I'm not telling you who they are. That's a part of an official investigation now."

She rose and began to clear away the remnants of their lunch as Caitlin rose as well to help. Carrigan pointed to the cupboard. "There are cupcakes and squares in there, Caitlin. Bring them out. I was in a mood to bake last night and got carried away, I fear."

Caitlin opened the cupboard, her mouth dropping open before she began to laugh. "Oh, my, Carrigan. Only slightly, I would say." She began to pull out pans of squares and cupcakes.

Carrigan blushed. "I guess I did. Baking is what helps me to relax sometimes. I don't eat it all. That's what I was doing this morning, Cameron. I had taken some over to Mrs. Fry who lives next door. She has grandkids who come all the time and is glad to have any baking I want to give her for them."

Chapter 14

Shoving his shop door closed behind him on the Monday morning following their meeting, Cameron sighed as he looked at the stack of orders waiting for him. His business was growing, almost too fast. He would need to add someone soon, and that was an unknown quantity he was so unsure of, especially right now.

He turned as he felt the breeze of the opening door and went to speak to the man who entered. Instead his hands rose into the air and he backed away, only stopping when he hit his reception counter.

The man who entered had pointed a gun at him, not saying a word. He walked towards Cameron, finally speaking.

"You're to come with me."

Cameron shook his head. "Nope. Sorry. Not happening. I don't go anywhere with someone who has a gun. People know that of me."

The man raised his weapon and Cameron crumpled to the floor from the blow

150

to his head with the gun butt, blood trickling from a wound on his forehead. The man shook his head before he pocketed his weapon, stooped and pulled Cameron to his feet, draping him over his shoulder, and heading back outside for his vehicle. He dumped Cameron into the back seat and drove off, not seeing the police vehicle heading his way.

Cameron was unaware that Tim hesitated, his eyes memorizing the plate number, and then he pulled over, running it. It came back clean, but he was still concerned. He searched Cameron's shop, not seeing him, but knowing his truck was outside. His keen eye spotted the few drops of blood on the floor and with an exclamation, he was back in his vehicle, racing for the address given for the plate number.

Cameron couldn't know that Tim found no one there. With no answer to his knock at the door, he was at a loss. He headed for a neighbour's house, coming back with little new information. But he just knew Cameron was there. He had to be. This was the address for the vehicle registration. He could feel his friend there somewhere, but just where?

Cameron, where are you? What has happened to you? He prayed for his friend's safety, not realizing that Cameron was indeed close by.

Cameron roused, slowly sitting up, a hand going to his head as it pounded with his effort to rise. He stared at the polished black shoes in his line of sight and went to raise his head, stopping as he felt the weapon once more digging into the back of head.

"Mr. Steele, we need to come to an understanding." The voice was low, harsh, and rough from years of misuse. "Your shop is exactly what we need to ship our merchandise."

"Not happening. I don't do crime." Cameron shifted away from the gun, still not looking up.

"Oh, I think you will. I brought you here to discuss our business arrangements with you. We will expect you to prepare a number of boxes to our specifications, have them ready in ten days. Someone will pick them up."

Cameron remained silent, even as the man continued to speak, a frown on his face. He should know the voice, he realized, but he couldn't place a name to it. The voice finally ceased and the squeak of shoe leather sounded in his ears as the man walked away. He waited, not knowing if he was alone or not, finally raising his eyes to search the room. Shed, he thought. An old garden shed, isn't it? He rose, staggering slightly from the lightheaded feeling he had, and then made his way to the door, feeling along it in the dimness, finding the latch and shoving through into the sunlight. He blinked, a hand coming up to protect his eyes, as the bright light caused his head to pound. He didn't hear a surprised voice calling his name, not until he felt a hand on his arm.

He spun, ready to strike back, when Tim spoke.

Tim could feel Cameron around the area. He called Cameron's phone, hearing a ringing and searching until he found it in a garden. He picked it up carefully, knowing Cameron would not have tossed it there. He turned as he heard a vehicle pull away, running for the driveway and seeing the vehicle he had been tracking pull away. He headed for the house once more, knowing Cameron was there somewhere. It was just too much of a coincidence. He saw Cameron opening the shed door and ran for his friend.

"Cameron? You are here. Something told me you were, even though I could get no answer from the house."

Cameron nodded. "I have no idea where I am. He knocked me out and I awoke here. Where am I, anyway?"

"At the old Rivers' estate. Why?"

Cameron shrugged as he walked with Tim towards the driveway. "Something about wanting me to build boxes to a certain specification. They gave me ten days to do so."

"As if you will." Tim reached for the paper. "Wow! They really are specific, aren't they?"

Cameron grabbed for the paper, shoving it into his pocket. "Let me put that away somewhere. I'm not doing them, but something tells me this is far from over."

"That I would say." Tim hesitated. "Carrigan called. She's received another object."

"What, this time?" When Tim didn't respond, Cameron looked at him. "Tim? How bad?"

"Bad enough that your uncle has said she goes nowhere alone. I have to head there once I'm done here. I just need to finish up with the team. I'll send them in to search the shed, but I doubt we'll find much."

"Maybe some footprints? I have no idea. Just get me to Carrigan." He paced, not liking having to wait for Tim. Finally, Tim walked back his way.

"Did she say what it was?" Cameron was anxious, almost willing Tim to speed.

"No, she didn't. Nor did Bill. He said he's called Mark, that Mark would be heading for her parents. It sounds as if he'll be sticking them away somewhere safe."

"I don't like the sounds of that, Tim. What next with these people?"

Tim shrugged as he pulled away from the house, heading for Carrigan. "I have no idea, Cameron, but today showed they are serious about making you work for them. Carrigan was right, you know."

"How?" Cameron studied his friend, seeing the concern on his face.

"She said all along they planned to make you work for them. That's what today was all about, wasn't it?"

"I guess." Cameron watched closely as Tim parked his patrol vehicle near his uncle's office, before he reached for the door handle, stopping as Tim laid a hand on his arm. "Tim?"

"Just be careful. That's all we ask, Cameron. For some reason, Carrigan has become a target of someone and that someone has you in his sights as well."

Cameron shrugged. "Without any name, we have nothing." He paused, a frown covering his face as he turned to Tim. "I know the man, Tim. I know his voice. I just can't place who it is. His man held a gun on me to keep me from looking up." He stared back out the window. "Why can't I place him?"

"Likely because it wasn't where you're used to seeing him. That happens. We see somewhere away from their usual haunt and can't put a name to them."

Tim stood for a moment eyeing his friend as Cameron asked the receptionist if Carrigan was in. Cameron turned back to where Tim was standing.

"She's not here. She headed for my place, she said. I don't like that, Tim."

"Alone?" At Cameron's nod, Tim grabbed his friend's arm and ran for his vehicle. "She's not supposed to do that."

Cameron nodded, then muttered under his breath as the traffic slowed in front of them, almost boxing them in. "What's up with this, Tim? We never have traffic jams."

"I know.   Something is weird about this."

Cameron caught slight movement to his right and turned his head, seeing the man who had struck him.   The man tipped an imaginary hat and then walked away, before Cameron could alert Tim. Cameron frowned. How close a watch would they keep on him? And where was Carrigan?

Carrigan had been unaware of what had happened to Cameron. She walked through the door of his shop, knowing his truck was outside, but not seeing him. She searched the shop, then stood, hands on her hips, and stared around. Where was he? He wouldn't just go off and leave his building unlocked, that she knew. She finally sighed to herself, resigned to the fact that he wasn't there, and headed for his office area, knowing he would have a pile of paperwork that he had not gotten to.   She sat, sorting through the material, lost in the task before many moments passed.

Hearing a sound, she started and then looked up, seeing the shadow of the door closing. She rose, cautiously peeking around the small wall and seeing a man standing near the counter before he walked towards her.

Cormac Steele stopped, his eyes on Carrigan, a puzzled look on his face. What was Carrigan doing here? And where was Cameron? He had asked his father to stop by that morning, but he was nowhere to be seen.

"Can I help you?" Carrigan's voice was low and he could hear the fear in it.

"It's okay. I'm Cormac Steele, Cameron's father. He asked me to stop in this morning. Is he around?"

Carrigan moved away from the desk, now recognizing Cormac. "No, actually, he isn't. I don't know where he is. I found the building unlocked when I got here, about an hour ago?" She looked at her watch. "Actually, two hours now. I have no idea where he is."

Cormac headed for the kitchen area, knowing that when Cameron returned, he would want coffee. He hesitated, not sure how to proceed with Carrigan, knowing that Cameron had been dating her but not talking to his father. That he would have to rectify, he thought.

"Carrigan, just why are you here? Aren't you supposed to be working?" Cormac stuck his head back around the wall separating the kitchen from the office area.

She nodded. "I was. Bill sent me home. I just couldn't stay there. I came here instead, looking for Cameron. I need to talk to him, but I'm not sure how."

"Words work." He grinned as she stared at him, mouth open before she snapped it closed. "He's really not that hard to talk to. I've been doing it for close to thirty years now with him."

"I know you have. You know him. I'm just learning how to have a conversation with him that doesn't involve him telling me I need to stay safe and to stop investigating." Her frustration came through in her words.

"Is that what he's been doing?" At her nod, he grinned again. "Of course, he would. He's a man. That what we men do." He disappeared from view and she heard the sound of water running, the rustle of the coffee filter, and then the click of the coffee machine. Cormac appeared once more, leaning against the wall. "So, which way do you want it?"

"Want what?"

"Your coffee, for starters?" He grinned once more as she shook her head at him. "No. With Cameron, it has always been very black and white. That's not how the world works. Both you and I know that." He stared at the floor for a moment. "You may not know that your Dad and I were close friends growing up. I was saddened when he decided to move away all those years ago. We never got to know your mom as well as we would have liked to." He raised his eyes that were so much like his son's.

Carrigan nodded before her mouth opened and words came out. "You look so much like Cameron." She blushed and wished she could take those very words back.

"I do? I'm honoured." Cormac turned in a circle, pretending to be on a runway. "But, I'm older. Shouldn't he look like me?"

His nonsensical talk was just what she needed and she broke down into laughter. "You got me there, didn't you? Yes, he looks like you. I said it that way as I know him, but not you."

"We need to fix that very thing. You must come for a meal. Morag has been after Cameron to bring you to dinner, but he keeps refusing."

"She hasn't! She has?" Carrigan's voice ended in a squeak, causing Cormac's laughter to ring through the shop once more.

"Just what is going on here?" Cameron's puzzled voice broke into their conversation, and both looked at him before back at one another, breaking out into fresh laughter.

"Good morning, son. I'm here at your request, but you weren't. Instead, I found a lovely young lady who has brightened my day." Cormac stared at his son's head for a moment, seeing the bandage on it, before he disappeared, returning with a tray of coffee. "Tim? You're here too? This can't be good."

Tim shook his head. "Not really, but why are you here? Carrigan? Why aren't you working?"

She threw up her hands and opened her mouth to speak, catching Cormac's eyes as she did so, seeing the grin he was trying very hard to hide. She laughed, shaking a finger at him. "Behave yourself, Mr. Steele. You're setting a bad example for your son."

"I am? I thought it was the other way around. That Cameron was setting a bad example for his father." He winked at her before they both grinned at each other, their teasing easing the unknown between them.

"Dad? Carrigan? What's going on? Or should I even ask?" Cameron reached for his cup of coffee, only to have his father swipe it from him. "Dad?"

"I'll give it back when you set a date to bring your lady here for dinner. Your mother's getting tired of waiting on that."

Cameron shrugged, his eyes searching Carrigan's face, seeing her agreement to that. "This week?"

"Not good enough. Set a day." Cormac was pushing it, he knew, but he also knew that Carrigan was enjoying his son's discomfort.

"This is Monday. Is tonight too soon?" Mischief sparkled in Carrigan's eyes as she watched Cameron sputter before he agreed, puzzlement in her mind as to what he had done to earn that bandage. She would ask him later, if the opportunity arose.

Tim choked on his coffee, sending himself into a coughing fit, and drawing the others' eyes to him.

"I forgot he was here." Carrigan was horrified at her forgetfulness. "Tim? Are you okay?"

He nodded as he wiped at his eyes. "I think so. Cameron, throw in the towel now. You'll never win with this lady." He watched as she laughed, but noted that the laughter didn't reach her eyes.

Cameron eyed her closely, seeing the shadows under her eyes and not just there. Shadows and fear lurked deep in her eyes. He hated that and wanted whatever was going on over for her.

"Carrigan?" When she looked up, he walked closer to her, perching on the corner on the desk. "What did you get in the mail?"

"It wasn't in the mail. It was hand delivered. No one saw anything or heard anything. It just showed up on the desk." She heard Tim's indrawn breath and nodded. "Just like some of the others."

"Just left at reception? No one around at the time?" When she shook her head, he turned and walked away, coming back to stand in front of her. "No one saw anything, is what you're saying? They're watching you too closely, Carrigan. Who is it?"

"If I knew, then I'd go after them and make them stop." She shoved back her chair and rose, standing toe to toe with Tim. "Yes, I would. Trust me. You don't mess with me."

Tim shook his head. "That is exactly what we don't want you to do."

Carrigan glared at him, seeing his concern for her behind his words. "I can't back away, Tim. Not any more. I'll do what

I need to in order to find the person or persons after me. I want to move on with my life and can't because of them." She brushed by him, almost running by the time she slammed the back door open and disappeared into the outside.

Cameron gave a low-voiced sound and ran after her, searching for her when he too hit the outdoors, finally seeing her perched on the picnic table. He walked slowly towards her, dropping to a seat beside her. He waited, finally stretching out his hand, palm side down in an invitation to her.

Chapter 15

Reaching for his hand after a while, Carrigan gripped it tightly, struggling to control the anger she was feeling, knowing anger did nothing, didn't solve anything, but not quite sure what she should be feeling. The few minutes she had spent talking to Cormac had helped her get back some perspective on life, but she knew her battle was far from over. Lord, please, I am just so tired. Tired of running from whoever it is. Tired of not having a life. Tired of being away from my parents. Tired of being scared. What else can I be tired of that You don't know about?

Cameron drew her closer to him, his hand warm and strong on hers, as he stared into the trees, not speaking, knowing she wasn't ready yet to say anything. He could wait, couldn't he, Lord? Wait for his lady to speak? For that is how he thought of her, his lady and his love.

Carrigan finally rested her head against Cameron's shoulder. "I'm sorry."

"Sorry for what? That you got angry? Just don't run away again. We can take your anger. It's you disappearing we'd have difficulty with." He suddenly grinned. "Did you really tell Dad we'd come for supper tonight? There's no way we can back out of it now."

She nodded, a small smile playing around her lips. "I did. I shouldn't have. Not without knowing if you had plans. I'll go tell him we can't." She made a motion to rise but his hand kept her in place.

"It's fine, Carrigan. I've been delinquent. Mom has asked, and I just kept putting it off, not knowing how you'd feel."

"You could have just asked me, Cameron, instead of assuming you knew how I'd answer." Her words had a bite to them, one he had not heard before. "Now, what are we to do about what I received?"

"The thing is, Carrigan, I don't know what you got. We never got that far. Tim didn't say, and you ran before you could tell me." He watched with concern as her eyes slid shut and panic and fear skittered across her face.

She nodded, a slow nod as she thought back over the day. "I'm tired of this, Cameron. I want it over but I don't know just how to do that."

"Tell me, Carrigan. What did you get this time?" He wrapped his arms around her, holding her as she shuddered from fear. "It has to be bad for you to be like this."

She nodded again, finally tilting her head to look up at him. "It is, Cameron. It's something else from my dollhouse. This time it was the baby's cradle. Only it wasn't empty." She closed her eyes and began to shake. "It had a tiny picture of me in it. Who is doing this?"

Cameron shook his head, horrified at the thought of Carrigan opening that package. "We need to find this person and put a stop to it. Have you any ideas who?"

She shook her head, her eyes on his face, seeing his concern and his fear for her. "I have no idea. I'm not even sure how it relates to that bank robbery any more, if it even does."

Cameron watched her beloved face, seeing the strain of what she was going through in it. *Lord, I want this to stop and I don't know how to do just that. I don't know how to protect her from the unknown.*

He spoke, not on what they had been talking about, but about his younger life, what it had been like growing up in Hope, his friends, his dreams, his plans. She watched his face, seeing the man he had become and knowing he wasn't just talking. He was letting her into his life in a way no one else ever had. She sighed to herself, knowing she would have to do the very same and not wanting to. She had become a very private person over the last few years, driven to be that by what she was going through.

"Thank you, Cameron. I needed this." She laid her head back on his shoulder. "Do we really have to move? I know you've got lots to do, and you did ask your father to stop by."

"He's fine with it if we don't talk until tonight. It wasn't anything really important. Not as important as you." He watched as her eyes slid shut and a single tear tracked down her face. He frowned. He didn't think he had seen her cry before. "Carrigan? Are you okay?"

She nodded, her hair brushing against his face. "I am, I think. Thank you. Now, let's go see what Tim wants. And no, I will not back away. Not any more. I can't, Cameron. Can you understand that?"

"I can. I just don't want you hurt." He felt her pushing against him and this time let her go, watching as she stepped down from the table and walked around the building. He waited for her to return. When she didn't, fear drove him to run after her, not seeing her as he rounded the building. He hadn't seen her car earlier and that scared him. Was she really walking?

He ran for his truck, pulling out his keys, accelerating quickly once he was behind the wheel. He drove towards her home, not seeing her on the way, and then circled back towards her office. There was no sign of her. Where is she, Lord? She can't have disappeared that quickly, could she?

He headed back for his shop, knowing he had to work, but his fear for Carrigan driving away all thoughts of his woodworking. His father looked up in surprise as he ran through the door.

"Cameron? What is going on? Carrigan ran past the window a while ago. Then we heard you take off. Tim went looking for Carrigan. I said I'd stay here in case either one of you came back."

"She was running? She walked away from me, said she wasn't backing down. Now, I can't find her." Cameron ran his hands through his hair, frustration and fear evident on his face. He paused for a moment beside the office desk, seeing the neat piles of invoices and shipping labels. "She was working when you got here, Dad?"

Cormac nodded from where he stood leaning against the table used for packaging. "She was. I think I scared her when I came in. I wasn't expecting her to be here. Just what all is going on, son? You asked me to meet you here. You weren't here but Carrigan was." He approached his son, stopping Cameron's restless movements with a hand to his shoulder. "And you have a cut on the side of your head."

"I was knocked out and taken to the old Rivers' estate, Dad. I didn't see who was in charge but I know him. I know his voice. I just can't place it."

Cormac's hand tightened on his son's shoulder. "You know him? It's someone from town?"

Cameron gave an abrupt nod. "It is. He gave me this." He pulled out the paper he had been handed. "They expect me to make these in a week. A week, Dad. That's all they gave me."

"Then, we'll have to do something within a week. We can't send you away, you're too busy." Cormac looked around at the stacks of unfinished boxes. "Looks as if I'll be working with you." He held up a hand at Cameron's protest. "It's not the first time. Since I retired from teaching, I need to do something. This fits, if you'll have me. I can work on the staining and the painting. Just put the details with each box. Are you lining the jewelry boxes with the velvet?"

Cameron and his father moved to the work bench as Cameron began to explain where he was on each box or chest. Cormac watched him closely, see the strain on his son's face, hearing it in his voice. Lord, take over here, please? I can't help him. None of us really can. Only You can. Bring his lady back safely, wherever it is she is.

Cameron finally stood back, his eyes on the boxes before shifting to his father, who worked away, concentration on his face. Cameron knew he was praying as well. He bit back a sigh. Sighing and moaning and complaining wasn't going to change the situation. He stepped away, his phone out, scrolling through. A message popped up. Carrigan has sent a text, apologizing for running, asking what time she should be ready that night. And yes, she was safe. Corbin had found her and taken her home. He had stayed, she said, to help her sort through some of the details of what she was finding out.

Cameron breathed a sigh of relief, looking up as he felt his father's hand on his shoulder once more.

"Cameron?"

"She's safe, Dad. Corbin found her and took her to her home. We're still on for tonight." He chewed at his lip, wanting to go to her, but knowing she was asking for some time, some quiet, and he had to grant her that.

Able to work away knowing that Carrigan was safe, Cameron lost himself in his creative work, rousing only when his father stopped by his work bench.

"Time to lock up, isn't it, Cameron? Your mother will expect you two in about an hour."

"What's that, Dad? That time already? Where did the day go?"

Cormac laughed as he pointed at the box Cameron was crafting. "On those. I'm not telling you what to do, Mr. Boss, but your lady is waiting for you. Don't keep her waiting."

Cameron nodded, watched his father walk away, and then tidied away his work, heading for his truck. He paused as he saw the envelope stuck to the driver's side window. He felt the angry beginning to grow

in him. Who now? Couldn't they just leave
him alone?

Chapter 16

Cameron turned back to the door as Carrigan opened it for him the following Sunday. He saw her face light up as she realized it was him. Was his love returned? He prayed it was, but he wouldn't ask. She had too much going on right now. Tim had talked to him. They were no further ahead in the investigation and that frustrated Cameron. He suspected Carrigan was forging ahead, but she wasn't saying much, and he knew exactly why. He needed to talk to her.

"All set?" He reached for her keys, locking her door, handing her back her keys, and then headed for his truck, her hand tight in his.

"Where are we off to, Cameron? It's Sunday, and we should be in church." She looked down at the dainty watch he had given her. "We still have some time until church starts."

He grinned as he tucked her into his truck and then ran around to slide behind the wheel.

"I have a surprise for you. A friend is preaching at a small church outside of town. I would like to take you to hear him, if you're agreeable."

"And if I'm not?" She was pushing him, she knew, but also knew she could do that. A small smile played around her mouth.

"Then we head for our own church. It's your decision, Carrigan."

"No, it's not just my decision, Cameron. You need to stop that. If we are a couple, then we make decisions together, not one or the other, unless there's danger. If you can't agree to that, then stop the truck and let me out now." She was getting frustrated and almost angry with him, knowing he was learning how to be part of a couple, just as she was.

"Okay, then, yes, I would like to go hear him."

"Then, fine, we'll go." She stared out the side window, not seeing the glances he kept throwing at her. She frowned as she saw a vehicle following them before it turned off. She was seeing people all over the place, she decided, and more than likely they had no interest in her.

She stood after the service, watching as Cameron spoke with his friend, a huge smile on his face. She frowned. Something was off here, she thought, before turning in a circle, not seeing anything, but knowing she was being watched. She didn't like that feeling at all.

Cameron's eyes found her and he drew his friend to meet her. They spoke for a few minutes before his friend was asked about another service and he turned away.

Cameron's arm around her, he led her from the small country church and to his truck. He stood for a moment, just holding her, feeling her lean into him.

"What happened, Carrigan?"

"Someone was watching me. I have no idea who."

Cameron tucked her into the truck and slowly circled it to his door, his eyes searching the crowd. He shook his head. He had no idea what he was doing or who he was looking for. He didn't have the kind of training that was needed for that.

He turned down a narrow country road, intending on heading back to Hope. Carrigan wasn't talking to him, lost in her thoughts. He reached for her hand, feeling her jump under his touch.

"Carrigan? Come back from wherever you are."

She turned, her eyes huge. "Cameron, I think I know who it might be. But he's dead. At least, that's what we've been told."

"Who, Carrigan?"

Before she could respond, they heard a cracking sound and a huge tree thudded to the road just in front of them. Cameron slammed on the brakes, the truck sliding around on the loose gravel before it slid off the side of the road into a shallow ditch, throwing the two of them around.

Carrigan sat for a moment, eyes huge, before she turned to Cameron. "Cameron? What happened?"

"I don't know but I don't like it. Come on. We're out of here." He pulled her from the truck, watching as she slid her purse strap around her shoulder and crisscross to her body. "Let's move into the trees. I'll call for help."

They moved away, hearing the sound of a vehicle approaching. Carrigan shook his head as Cameron went to walk back to the truck, shoving at him.

"No." She hissed at him in a low voice. "This didn't just happen. I think it was planned."

"But how?" His voice was equally low. "How did they know?"

"They plan ahead, is what they do. I thought someone had been following us when we set out, but they turned off. I guess they were following us after all."

He wrapped his arms around her and drew her back into the trees, hearing the steps approaching them and the curses and foul language uttered as they weren't found. Carrigan buried her head against him, shudders running through her. To what extent would this person go to, she wondered? Lord, we need You.

Carrigan raised her head, a frown on her face, as she listened to the voices. She thought she knew one, but without seeing the man, she couldn't be certain. She would need to talk to her father. He had known the man at one time.

Cameron drew her back further into the woods, his head turned as he listened to the thrashing and commotion coming from behind them. He wanted to get Carrigan to safety, but his truck was behind him and he knew from experience he wouldn't have any cell service. It was spotty at best in this area, and he didn't want to take a chance on stopping and being caught.

He turned his head for a moment, eyes searching as he heard the noise getting closer, and then took a step forward, not finding anything under his foot. He gave a cry, his arms tightening around Carrigan as they fell, hitting the slope hard and sliding down. Her scream rang through the air before their downward motion stopped. He lay still for a moment, his breath gone, pain radiating through him.

Carrigan raised her head, her eyes searching the edge of the slope before she struggled from his arms and pulled him to his feet and away from sight.

"Cameron? Are you okay?" Her voice was low, concern lacing it.

He finally nodded, the pain wracking his body increasing in severity. "I think so. I hurt." He sank to the forest floor, not caring that it was damp and slightly muddy. His head dropped to his upraised knees.

She dropped to her own knees, her hands assessing him. "Did you hit your head?"

He nodded. "I think I did. The back of it hurts. Hey! Be careful!" He jerked away as her fingers gently probed through his hair.

"Ssh! We're trying to be quiet, you know." She stepped away, watching the trail they left. "We need to get out of here, Cameron. Can you walk?"

He shrugged, pulling himself to his feet. "I may need your help." He studied the area and then the sky. "I want to get back to my truck. If we go this way, we should be able to make it back."

"But won't they be waiting? It's what I would do." She followed, her hand on his back, watching him carefully as he stumbled on occasion, finally drawing him to a stop. "Cameron. You need to rest. I think we're okay right now." She felt her phone vibrating. "I thought you said we wouldn't have cell service."

"I said it's spotty. Who's trying to reach you?"

She pulled out her phone, searching her messages. "It's your Dad. He couldn't reach you. He said Mark is looking for us." She bit at her inner cheek, worry on her face before determination coloured it. "We'll make it, Cameron. Do you want me to call for help?"

He shook his head. "Not yet. The road should be right ahead. Come on. And pray that my truck is still there and drivable." He felt for his phone. "My phone's still in the truck."

She nodded, knowing what he was hinting at. "Let's go then. Just be careful. If you fall again, I can't pick you up." She smirked as he stared at her, before he shook his head and reached for her hand.

Hand in hand, they approached the road, staying in the shadows as they watched. No one seemed to be around.

"Stay here, Carrigan, and I mean it. Let me get to the truck and get it backed up. There's got to be somewhere I can turn it around. And if someone approaches me, run and hide. Find a spot you can hunker down and call for help if you can."

"There was a small laneway back a bit. It's overgrown somewhat but I think it would work."

He studied her face for a moment, then, giving into an impulse, he leaned forward and kissed her. He turned and moved quickly towards his truck, not seeing the look of first shock, then acceptance, then another emotion she was afraid to name, run across her face. She held her breath as he slid into the truck after walking around it and ducking down to check underneath.

She ran for the open door when he paused beside her, quietly pulling the door closed. "Everything was okay?" When he didn't respond, his body turned as he watched through the back window, finally able to turn the truck and then accelerating away from the area. "Cameron? I asked you a question."

"I know you did. And no, it wasn't. There's something odd about the truck and I want to find Tim. Let him go over it. I think they've been tracking us somehow."

She sat back, her hand gripping her seatbelt until the knuckles turned white. "Cameron? Is that how they knew?"

"I suspect so." He nodded and then wished he hadn't done that very thing. His head was beginning to pound. He pulled over. "Can you drive us home, Carrigan? I've got a brutal headache."

She stared at him. "Not home. To the hospital. You're getting yourself assessed. And if I'm driving, I get to say where we go."

Too sore and hurting to argue, he simply slumped back into the passenger seat, his eyes sliding closed against the glare of the sunlight. *Lord, I need to not be hurt. I need to keep Carrigan safe. I have all those orders* too. He sighed to himself. Here he was, telling God what to do. He knew better than that. God would provide, his father would tell him, and he knew to be a fact. That had been proven over and over again.

She watched the doors to the examination rooms, knowing that she couldn't be back there with him. She had called Cormac, reaching his voice mail. Tim had appeared and then taking the keys to Cameron's truck, disappeared with it. So, she thought, I'm basically stuck here, no transportation, no word on Cameron. Not how I pictured my day. Not at all.

She looked up as she heard her name called and rose to walk towards the nurse.

"It's okay, Carrigan. Cameron asked for you to come back. He said you'd be pacing." The nurse smiled as Carrigan shook her head.

"No, not pacing. I'm too tired to do that. How is he?"

The nurse shrugged. "The doctor will be with him soon. He'll explain everything to you both. Right in here."

Carrigan hesitated for a moment, her eyes tracking back to the door, a frown on her face. Even here, she felt watched. Why?

Lord, I've had enough. I want this over but it's in Your hands.

She turned to find Cameron, who lay on the stretcher, his eyes closed, hands resting on the top of the light blanket covering him. She walked softly towards him, seeing his eyes open and search until they found her. His hand reached out for her.

"I asked them to let you come back here. I didn't want you out there on your own." He groaned as he shifted.

"Have they said anything yet?"

He shook his head, pain crossing his face. "Not yet. They don't think I broke anything though."

"That's good. But Cameron? Your orders? What do I do to help you?"

He watched her beloved face, seeing the emotions playing across it. He reached up to touch it. "You can help just by being you, by being there. Dad's been working with me the last few days, doing the painting and staining. Thanks to his help, I've managed to get caught up." He groaned again as he thought of the orders waiting to be mailed. "Except they are ready to be mailed and I just don't have the energy to do that."

"I talked to Caitlin. She can free up her evenings for the next couple of days. I can do the same. Bill heard and told me to work part time for him and part time for you until you were caught up. So, it's covered." She watched as his eyes slid shut in thankfulness. "Did you really think I'd let you down, not when you saved me today from who knows what?" She could feel hurt and anger rising in her and knew better. Cameron really hadn't gotten to know her, she thought.

Cameron watched her face, slight amusement in his eyes. "Draw in the claws, Carrigan." Her mouth dropped open at his words. "I meant what I said. Draw in the claws. I know you won't let me down. That's not what friends do. But you work for my uncle, and that should be your first priority."

She shook her head, frustration evident on her face. "That's not what friends do. They take care of one another. If that's how you view our friendship, then maybe I should just leave." She withdrew from him, turning to walk away, when he lunged for her, wrapping his arms around her and drawing her down to a sitting position on the stretcher. "Cameron! Let me go!" She struggled to escape, but his strength kept her tight to him.

He looked up as he heard a sound at the door, and Mark appeared.

"Mark? You're here? What is going on?" Cameron didn't let go of Carrigan, just eased his grip a bit.

"Looking for you two. I didn't expect to find you in the hospital, though, Cameron. Care to explain?"

The young couple shared a glance before Carrigan spoke, telling Mark what had transpired, just not sharing her feelings. Those were in such an upheaval, she just didn't know which end was up where they were concerned. And then there was Cameron's kiss. She needed to talk to him about that too.

"I see. I tried to find you earlier, but no one seemed to know where you were. That's not likely a good idea." He watched, amusement on his face, as Carrigan sputtered, knowing exactly what she was going to say.

Instead, she paused, her eyes on Cameron. "I think I know who it is, but he's dead, Mark. How can that be?" She sighed, her eyes closing against her fear and the pain she was feeling herself. She hadn't walked away without getting hurt either. She just refused to acknowledge it.

"Carrigan?" When she didn't respond, Cameron touched her cheek, causing her to jump. "Who do you think it is?"

She shook her head. "I need to talk to Dad first. He would know." She turned to Mark. "Mom and Dad?"

"They are safe, Carrigan. I've made sure of that. Here's another number to call them at. I don't want you using their normal numbers." Mark handed her a slip of paper that she glanced at, then tucked into her purse. "Now, about you two. Go over, step by step, what happened."

Cameron did just that, his eyes on Carrigan as she watched Mark, leaving out the bit about his kiss. He sighed to himself. He had overstepped, he knew, and would need to apologize.

Mark asked the questions he needed to clarify what they had said, then tucked his notepad away into a pocket, leaning against the foot of the stretcher, watching as the two in front of him tried hard not to look at one another. He shook his head, remembering what it had been like when he was first dating his wife.

He finally walked away, taking one look back at Cameron, a frown on his face as he watched Carrigan. She was up to something, he knew. Please, Lord, keep her safe. Keep her in that hollow of Your Hand. That man there would be devastated if something happened to her.

Chapter 17

Carrigan looked up from her desk a week later, hearing footsteps heading her way, and dreading who it might be. It had been a horrible week, she decided, too many thefts, too many break-ins, too much property damage. Bill's investigators were stretched thin. He informed that he didn't want them working overtime, that they would do what they could during working hours. They would burn out otherwise. She had nodded, a frown on her face. Just what was happening here, Lord? I came here to Hope to be safe, to find a place I could plant roots. Now, it seems as if I'm going to have to go back on the run.

Cameron appeared in her doorway and walked to sit on the edge of her desk, shifting papers over so he could do just that. He thanked God daily for His protection and the quick healing he had undergone. Nothing broken in his fall, just a lot of bruising. He was grateful that Carrigan hadn't been hurt, at least, he didn't think she had. She wouldn't say.

"Cameron? It's daytime. What are you doing here?"

"Dad kicked me out of the building. Told me to go find a lovely young lady and take her to lunch." He grinned as she shook her head at him, an answering smile on her face. "Can I tempt you to run away for an hour or so?"

She rose, reaching for her purse. "I could use a break. It's been a hectic week."

He grabbed for her hand, stopping her in her tracks, his other hand coming up to caress her cheek. "We need to talk at some point, Carrigan."

She froze in place, her eyes huge as she watched him. "We do. I just don't know when."

"Soon, Carrigan. Very soon. I would like to take you out for a dress-up dinner. We've never got to that yet, you know."

She nodded, knowing it was inevitable now that they talked. "I see. Well, then, I guess we must, mustn't we?" She smiled and turned away, slipping her hand from his, to go let Bill know she would be out of the office for an hour or so. She hesitated as she saw him on the phone and turned to leave, his eyes catching her motion and his hand motioning for her to stop.

"Carrigan!" His voice was somber as he hung up the phone. "I was just going to come and find you. That candlestick you found at Cameron's? It didn't belong to you after all."

"It didn't? Well, that's a relief. But whose was it?"

"That is an interesting point. Tim just called. His mother's sister had the dollhouse that had been their mother's. She was away for a few months and just returned home. She called Tim to come take a look through her house as she thought someone had been in. That was the only thing taken. She had it in a display case with some other miniatures."

She stared at him, not having heard Cameron come up behind her, a frown on his face at the length of time she was taking. She jumped as she felt his arms come around her, pulling her back to him.

"Uncle Bill?" Cameron was puzzled, and even more so once his uncle had explained. "That makes no sense, Uncle Bill. Why involve Tim and his family?"

"To throw us off. That's why." Carrigan's eyes were narrowed. "There's something more to this than what we think. I've been researching but getting nowhere. Mark and Tim have both been looking into things for me."

"You said you needed to ask your father about someone." Cameron leaned around her to look into her face, seeing the fatigue lining it.

"I did. He's promised to find out what he can, but he's stuck away somewhere and he has to be very careful."

"Did he give the name to Mark?"

She shook her head, her eyes on Bill. "No, not yet. We're trying to do it unofficially. Corbin talked to my Dad. I have no idea how he got that number, but he's researching things as well. He needs to stop."

Cameron began to laugh, drawing her attention to him. "Might as well tell the sun to stop shining. Once Corbin's got his teeth into something, he doesn't give up."

He watched as she drew in a deep breath, her eyes resting on Bill, before she literally shook herself and then turned back to him. "You said something about lunch, Mr. Steele? I will have you know the day's wasting, and I, for one, am starved."

Bill starting laughing. "I think you just got told. Go on. Get out of here." He continued to laugh as, nose in the air, Carrigan brushed by Cameron and headed for the front door, Cameron standing in shock for a moment before he shook his head and ran after her.

Carrigan studied the man sitting across from her as he perused the menu at his aunt's. She knew he was doing that to avoid a conversation with her and that she would not allow any more.

"Cameron?" When he looked up, a smile on his face, she continued. "We need to talk. It's been almost a week. And we've been avoiding something."

He sobered, laying aside the menu, knowing his aunt would just order for him anyway. "We do. I need to apologize, Carrigan. I shouldn't have kissed you, not without your permission."

She nodded. "Thank you, Cameron. That means a lot, but it's okay. I think I wanted you to." She blushed, her eyes on her hands, jumping when his reached for hers and tugged at them gently, making her look up at him. She drew a deep breath, seeing what he wanted to say but wouldn't vocalize on his face, and knew her face responded. "Where do we go from here?"

"Well, let's see. We do need to return to work." He smirked as she smacked his hand before he clasped hers again. "Let's go out tonight, do our dress-up dinner and then talk. We've been skirting the issue and we can't any more."

Later that night, Cameron once more reached for her hand, sensing tension and stress in her grip.

"Carrigan? Are you okay?"

She nodded, a distant look on her face. "I think so. Just an odd sensation today. Like something's about to break loose and I can't stop it. You know, like when a dam gives way and washes everything away in the water's path?"

He shuddered, having felt something similar. "I know what you mean. But what would it be?"

She shook her head, her eyes on the horizon. "I have no idea. Dad got back to me about that man, but I need to talk to Mark before I say anything. I'm just so confused. I talked to Tim, but that didn't help him out at all."

He drew her down to a bench, the setting sun reflecting off their faces. "Let's forget about that for a moment. You did say we needed to talk."

"We do. Cameron, I have no idea where this is taking me, taking us. I think we might need to stay away from one another for a while. I don't want to see you hurt again. I care too much for you."

Cameron had known that was exactly what she was going to say. "That is not happening, Carrigan. We're in this together, so get that straight. I don't want anything to happen to you, but if, God forbid, it does, I want to be the one who is there."

She stared at him, knowing she would not be able to talk him out of it, and knowing the only way she could control the situation would be to walk away. And that was just what she didn't want to do, couldn't do. "So, where does that leave us then?"

"As a dating couple? Feeling our way to something more?" He reached to draw her close, tucking her to his side. "I love you, Carrigan. I don't expect you to feel the same, not yet any way. But I just want you to know how I feel."

She studied him closer, seeing the sincerity in his face and hearing it in his voice. "Thank you, Cameron. I need to think and pray over this. I thought you did, but I wasn't sure."

An hour later, they rose, heading for his truck, not seeing the man who approached from behind them and walked on by them, his eyes intent on them. If they had, perhaps things might have gone differently. Only God would know that, and they just weren't paying attention to the others around them, only themselves.

Cameron slid behind the wheel of his truck, his eyes on the muted lights of Carrigan's house. He hadn't not wanted to walk away from her, feeling danger lingering around them, danger he had no idea who from. They planned to spend Saturday together, and that would have to do, he thought. She had not turned down his suit, he was to note, but he knew she would have to think it through. That was who she was, not running into any rash decisions.

Carrigan listened to Cameron drive away and then turned to kick off her shoes and head for the kitchen. She had research to do and needed her coffee to keep her awake.

She finally sat back, staring at her watch. It was well towards morning, but she finally felt like she was making progress in her hunt. She sent her file on to both Mark and Tim, asking them to research in an official manner now. If she was right, hopefully soon, she prayed, things would be resolved. But a little voice inside her asked if she wasn't right, then what? And if she was right, then what? Would she really be safe at all? Lord, You promise. You promise to keep us safe, to keep us in the hollow of Your hand, under the shadow of Your wings. I need that so desperately, Lord, right now. And Cameron. Dear sweet Cameron, whom I love so deeply. Keep him safe as well, Lord.

She finally rose, heading for bed, when she stopped, her head tilting as she heard a scraping sound from the back deck. She tiptoed that way, leaning carefully to look out. Nothing showed, but that didn't mean something or someone hadn't been there. She would wait until morning and check it out.

She headed for her back deck when she arose a few hours later, cautiously cracking open the door and peeking out, finally emerging to search her deck, finding nothing. She shrugged. It must have been that cat again, she thought, not seeing the box sitting near her planter.

Chapter 18

Cameron locked the truck behind them on Saturday morning, turning to reach for Carrigan's hand. He had brought her to a neighbouring town, looking for inspiration for his boxes. He was always challenged artistically here in this town.

Her eyes roamed the area, seeing the quaintness of it, but also searching for trouble. She didn't think they'd get to enjoy a day away without something happening. She hated feelings like the one she had, because they almost always came true. Lord, I'm claiming Your protection today. Please, keep us safe?

Cameron pulled her with him into an antique shop, his eyes alight with pleasure as he studied the wood crafts that he found. A pencil and pad in hand, he rapidly sketched ideas until Carrigan's hand reached to stop him.

"Cameron? Use your camera on your phone. That way you can take multiple pictures and sort through them." She laughed at the blank look on his face that turned to astonishment and then glee.

"I would never have thought of that. I'm so glad you're here." He reached to hug her, his arm staying around her shoulders as they left the store. He glanced at the sky. "Listen. It will soon be lunch, but there is one place I want to show you."

"One place?" She protested. "My feet are sore, Cameron. How far of a walk is it?"

He hugged her tighter to him. "I could always carry you." He laughed as she blushed and looked away from him. "I'm sorry, not. It's only a few minutes."

She stood at the base of the building, her head tilted back to look at the clock above them. "This is seriously tall, you know. We can go in?"

Cameron laughed at the look on her face. "We can. They have areas blocked off we can't enter, but we can go to the top."

She frowned at him. "And just how many stairs are there?"

He shook his head, reaching for her hand and pulling her with him, oblivious to the men standing near the neighbouring building, their eyes on the couple. "Some. Come on. The view is worth the climb."

She stood at the top of the stairs, staring back down. "Some, he says. Some? Just how many were there?" She waved her hands in front of her. "Don't tell me. I don't want to know how many I have to walk back down."

He laughed even as he drew her to the edge of the walkway around the clock workings. "It's easier going down. Look!" He pointed through the glass to the surrounding view. "Isn't that worth it? Today's a perfect day to see."

She stared around at the scenery and then lifted her eyes to the horizon, her mouth open until she remembered to close it. She studied the hills in the distance and thought of the verse about her help coming from the hills when she lifted her eyes to them. She closed her eyes briefly, sadness flitting across her face, not seeing Cameron's eyes on her.

"Carrigan?   Are   you   okay?" Cameron's soft voice reached her and she nodded even as he touched her face with the back of his fingers.

"I am, thank you for asking. The hills always remind of where I get my help."

He turned his head to follow her line of sight. "I never think of that. Thank you. I have a feeling we're far from done and that only God will get us through."

"I know He's the only one, Cameron." She turned to watch the clock workings as they moved around the walkway. "This is fascinating. Thank you for bringing me up here."

"Even if you do have to walk down all those stairs."

She laughed even as she nudged him with her shoulder. "Even with that. I needed today. Thank you." She reached to hug him.

Cameron frowned as he heard a sound from the bottom of the stairs and drew Carrigan away from that staircase. He knew there was another one, a hidden one, that they could use. The clock mechanic had shown it to him one day.

"Mr. Steele? We know you're up there. We need to talk, Mr. Steele."

Cameron drew in a deep breath and began to feel along the wall, finding the catch to the door, and shoving Carrigan into the opening that appeared, following her and drawing the door closed behind them. A finger to her lips kept her silent even as they heard the men walking around and talking, curses beginning to fill the air as they didn't find Cameron.

Carrigan wrapped her arms around Cameron, desperate to feel his presence close to her in the darkness. With him, she felt safe. His hand moved from her face and she felt him grasp her hand and lead her forward.

"Be careful. There's a step right in front of me. It's a circular metal staircase. Here. Put your other hand here. That's the top of the railing. I'll hold your other hand."

Cameron led her down carefully, his eyes shooting glances behind them every once in a while. They were far enough away that they could no longer hear the men. He reached the bottom of the steps and felt for the door, knowing it would open with the panic bar and that they could get out.

A hand stopped his movement towards the bar. "Cameron? What if they are waiting outside for us?"

He hugged her again. "It's a chance we'll have to take. This opens up behind some tall bushes, so they shouldn't be able to see us." He cracked open the door, momentarily blinded by the light, before leading her out and away from the building. He searched but didn't see the men, but that didn't mean they weren't still there. He knew that only too well.

"Cameron?" When he turned to look at her, Carrigan shrugged. "What was that all about?"

"About me not making those boxes for them, I suspect. I have refused. I have the plans and specifications they gave me locked away safe. But I have no intention of aiding them in smuggling." He drew her with him towards his truck. "I'm sorry, sweetheart. This was meant to be a happy day, not this."

"It's been good, even though you made me walk up all those stairs." She drew out the last three words, hiding a grin as his head shot around and his eyes narrowed as he watched her before he grinned.

"There weren't that many, now were there? In you go. We'll find somewhere to have some lunch and then decide what we want to do for the rest of the day."

She watched behind them for a while, not seeing anyone. "Did we lose them, do you think?"

He shrugged. "I suspect for now. Unfortunately, they know where we live and work. We can't hide totally from them."

"No, we can't." She turned to stare out the side window, her voice dying away as she thought through what she knew and what she surmised. "Do we know the man who's behind this, Cameron?"

"I think we do. I just have no idea who it is. Corbin said he had an idea as to who it was but he hasn't said anything in the last few days."

Late that afternoon, Cameron drew up in front of Carrigan's house, coming around to open the door for her and walk her up to her door. She paused, her eyes on his face, before she reached to hug him.

"Thank you, Cameron. I needed today. It was good to get away and do something fun."

He smiled, a hand coming up to run down her cheek. "I'm glad you could go. It's always better having someone to do things with."

She nodded, then turned to enter her home, locking up as he waited before she watched him walk away, a sense of foreboding coming over her. Now, what is this about, Lord? Are things really going change that much? I so enjoyed today. I just didn't want it to end, but it had to.

She walked through to her office, dropping down into her chair, and pulling off her loafers. Her feet were sore, but she decided it had been worth it. She was falling deeper in love with Cameron but still wasn't sure of his feelings for her. She knew he had some, just by his actions and his treatment of

her, cherishing her like she was beloved by
him.

Chapter 19

Frowning at Carrigan's door the next morning, Cameron pounded at the wood, knowing she said she would be ready for him. He stepped back, staring around, then walked across the porch to the front window. Hands cupped around his face, he leaned close, trying to see in. The drapes were open, but he had trouble seeing through the lacy sheers she had hung up. He sighed. Where was she?

He stepped from the porch and walked around the house, to the back door, finding it locked as well. He reached for his phone, scrolling through his messages and then checking his voice mail. Not a word, he thought, and this is not like her. She would have called me, or at least sent a text message, if she wasn't going to church today, or was even running late and would meet me there.

He walked around the house, trying the windows, knowing that if he found one open, he would have to debate with himself whether to enter or not.

He turned for the garage, a frown on his face. Now, why hadn't he checked there before? Maybe she had been called out and in the rush had forgotten to send a message. He stared through the dusty window at her vehicle, fear suddenly rising within him. He turned back to the house, this time searching harder for a way to enter, finally stepping back, knowing she had locked everything up the night before. He had heard the front door lock snap closed behind her.

He reached for his phone, calling his uncle, hoping he would know where she was. When Bill answered in the negative and said he'd be right over, he had a key, Cameron breathed a sigh of relief. Maybe, just maybe, she was still sleeping, or had fallen and couldn't get up. But he frowned as he stared at the front door. That didn't sound right, not at all.

Lord, where is my lady? Is she safe? Will she come back to me? Please, dear Lord, she talked about looking to the hills for her help. I have to do that. I have to run to that strong tower You are and be safe for her. Lord, I just know this is all related to what's been going on. But where is she? Please, Lord, bring her back to me.

He bit at his lip as the tears clouded his vision for a moment before he blinked and then straightened up taller. He would not give in to despair. She had to be inside, he kept insisting to himself.

Bill shut his car door, watching Cameron as he sat on the front steps, head in his hands, a dejected look about him. He shook his head. Just where are you, Carrigan? Don't disappear on my boy. Don't do that to him.

"Still no sign of her?" Bill's voice startled Cameron, causing him to jump to his feet, a wild look on his face.

"Not a one, Uncle Bill. You're sure you have a key?"

Bill gave a grim smile. "I do, son. She made me take one, just in case, she said." He headed for the door, opening it and stepping through. "Stay here, Cameron. Let me go through first."

Bill searched the house, seeing Carrigan's purse on her desk where she left it the day before, her keys next to it, her shoes laying just as they had landed when she kicked them off. He searched further, not seeing any sign of her, or any sign of any trouble. It was like she had disappeared in thin air, he thought. He paused, hand running along his jaw, before he pulled out his phone. This was over his head, he thought, making a call he never thought and had fervently prayed that he never would have to make. Carrigan had become like a daughter to him and his wife.

Cameron stood where his uncle had left him, a hopeful look on his face, that disappeared as he saw his uncle walking towards him, phone to his ear. His heart dropped within him even as his face changed from hope to despair.

"Uncle Bill?" Cameron spoke as soon as Bill pocketed his phone. "Is she here?"

Bill looked with compassion as his nephew, shaking his head. "No, she's not, son. Not at all. Her purse is on her desk as are her keys. Shoes under the desk that I think she just kicked off. She's not here, son. Her bed hasn't been slept in, unless she had made it up again."

Cameron blew out a breath. "That's bizarre. She can't just have disappeared." He moved to walk past his uncle until Bill's hand stopped him and turned him around, guiding him out the door and to his own vehicle.

"No. We're not going back in there, Cameron. I've put in a call and someone from the police will be here shortly. We have to let them go through the house first."

Cameron slumped back against his uncle's car, watching the activity as the police entered the house, some officers searching outside and in the garage. "I need to tell them I was trying the windows on the outside, Uncle Bill. My footprints might be in the garden. I never thought. I didn't know. I just……." His voice died away.

"We know that, Cameron. Now, they'll come and take a statement from you once they've had a chance to assess the situation." Bill looked around as he heard footsteps and saw Cormac and Corbin heading their way. "Your Dad and brother are here."

Cameron's eyes slid shut. "Thank you. Lord, please?" His words died away with that muttered prayer, even as he was flanked by his father and brother, who stood, silent, just waiting, just there for him.

Cameron looked up as he saw a pair of feet stop just in his line of sight and saw an officer standing there. "Gerry?"

"Cameron. What can you tell me? Your uncle said you were here first and could get no response from Carrigan, is it?"

Cameron nodded, his eyes shifting from Gerry to the house. "We were to go to church. I was picking her up. When I couldn't get an answer, I searched for a way in. I even checked the garage and saw her car. That's when I called Uncle Bill, wondering if he had a key. I didn't go past just inside the front door. Uncle Bill wouldn't let me." He looked at Gerry, hope in his eyes. "Did you find her?"

Gerry shook his head. "Sorry, Cameron. Not yet. We're still working the scene. Would she have gone anywhere that you know of?"

Cameron shook his head. "No. Not without her purse. If she had been called into work, or something had come up, she would have called me or at least sent me a text message. I received neither." He felt his father's hand on his shoulder. "Where is she?"

"That's what we are working to determine, Cameron." Gerry looked around as he heard his name called. "Listen. We need your statement and your uncle's. That means we'll need you to come downtown." He held up a hand at Cameron's protest. "Today, Cameron. In fact, your Dad can take you. Leave Corbin here to irritate us if you must." He gave Corbin, a good friend, a quick grin.

Cameron finally nodded, watching as Gerry walked away before he turned and followed his father to his car, stopping to look back at the house. He had a bad feeling about this, he decided. *Lord, where is she? Is she okay? Is she still alive?*

Cormac watched closely as his son talked with the officer assigned to take his statement, worry in his heart. He reached for his phone, intending on calling someone, but just who, he had no idea. He stared down at his phone, frustration evident as Cameron stopped beside him.

"Dad?"

"You're all done, Cameron?" At Cameron's nod, he stood, walking out with Cameron to his car. "You want to go back to her house, don't you?"

"I guess, Dad. I don't know where else to go." He turned in a circle. "Someone's watching us, but I can't see who it is."

"Is this what you've been talking about, what's been happening to you and Carrigan? Why didn't you say more?"

Cameron shrugged. "Because we didn't see who it was. The police can't work on hunches and feelings." He was frustrated and bit back angry words. "Can you take me to my shop? I want to check there to make sure she hasn't walked there."

"Now why would she do that, if you had planned to pick her up at her house?"

Cameron shook his head. "I have no idea, Dad. I'm just grasping at straws, I think, and hoping I find her." He searched the streets as his father drove through town, hoping against hope, praying that he would see her and not doing that. He felt his heart sinking. Lord, please? Where is she?

He locked his shop door behind him. His father had been right. Carrigan was not there. He climbed back into his father's car, pulling out his phone and thumbing through his messages, pausing at an unknown number showing.

"Dad, do you know this number? The call came in late last night."

Cormac took a quick look. "No, but the area code is from here. Give the number to Gerry. He can run it and see if it leads anywhere." He shot a look at his son, seeing the worry and fear he was trying so hard to hide. "Let your emotions out, son. It never pays to hold them in. What time did that call come in?"

Cameron took another look at it. "Around 10:30, it says. I never heard the phone ring." He paused in his words, searching his memory for what he was doing at that time. His eyes slid shut. "I had left my phone in the kitchen and headed for bed. I never heard it ring."

"Don't beat yourself up too much, son. It happens. You don't know that it was her. It could have been someone wanting to contact you about your work."

"At that time of night?" Cameron bit back the words he wanted to say, knowing his father didn't deserve them. "But what if it wasn't?" He was convinced it had been Carrigan, but why that number? Why not her own phone?

Cameron approached Corbin back at Carrigan's, hope on his face. "Corbin?"

Corbin composed himself before he turned to face Cameron, catching his father's eyes and giving a small shake of his head.

"She's not here, Cameron. They think she disappeared last night. What time did you two get back?"

Cameron shrugged, then jammed his hands into his jacket pockets. "I don't know for sure, but it was around six or thereabouts. I was home by 6:30." He watched as Gerry moved his way. "There's no sign of her, is there?"

Gerry paused, his eyes searching Cameron's face, before he spoke. "No, she's not. Her security system was activated around 11, so she must have left then."

Cameron held out his phone. "Can you check this number? I don't know it, but it came through around 10:30 last night."

Gerry jotted down the number, promising to look into it. "How was she when you left last night?"

"Tired. Dusty. We had spent the day in Oak City, climbed the clock tower, had lunch." He paused, his eyes sliding closed. "How could I forget? Cameron! Get ahold of yourself!"

"Cameron? What are you talking about?" His father's voice cut through his remonstrations to himself.

"When we were in the clock tower, two men climbed up and called for me. I took her down the access stairs and out. They wanted me to produce those boxes, Dad, the ones I'm not making."

Gerry's hand paused as he was jotting notes. "What boxes?"

"Someone wanted me to make boxes to a certain specification. I have refused. Now,

I wonder if they've taken Carrigan to make me do just that."

Gerry gave a sound of frustration. "And you didn't think to talk to us?"

"Gerry." At Cormac's voice, Gerry looked his way. "Cameron talked to Tim and together they filed a report, along with a report that Cameron was kidnapped from his shop one day. These are the report numbers. Take a look at them." Cormac watched Cameron closely, knowing he was going to have to get him out of there. "If you're done, can we leave? I know we'll have to come back for Cameron's truck, though."

"Yeah, you can leave. Just let me know if you hear anything at all."

Cameron gave an abrupt nod, then spun, heading for Corbin's car. Corbin had a quick word with his father and uncle and then ran to catch up with his brother, his key fob unlocking the doors.

Cameron slid into the passenger seat, his eyes on the house and then the garage, a frown in place. "Corbin. Where is she?"

"That's what we need to figure out. I'm taking you to my place." He held up a hand. "Don't argue, okay? It just makes sense. I can research better on my own computer. I have the programs and files I need there."

"And just what files would they be?" Cameron's voice bit back at his brother, anger and worry edging his words.

"Carrigan asked me to research a man from years ago. I haven't been able to even find a photo of him, which is strange. I should be able to find even a school picture."

"That is strange. Any idea why?"

Corbin shrugged as he pulled to a stop in his driveway, his hand going out to stop his brother's movements. "Wait a moment, Cameron. I have no idea what she wanted or why. She didn't say. And yes, I should be able to find even an elementary school photo and can't. He's taken pains to hide himself and hide himself well. That's not why I stopped you. We need to pray for Carrigan and for you and for the investigators. Mark is heading this way later, he said. He was going to speak with her parents."

Cameron nodded, then reached for the door handle, his hand pausing. "I wish I could figure this out, Corbin. I really do. I just don't know where she is or who has her." He gave his brother a look that showed all the pain and fear and hurt he was feeling. "Did she just walk away? Leave everything behind her, including me?"

"She's not that type, Cameron. She wouldn't do that to you. You know better." Corbin paused, pursing his lips as he tapped the steering wheel with the fingers of one hand, deep in thought. "No. She wouldn't walk away. She cares too much for you. Anyone who is around you two can see that."

"Thanks, Corbin. I thought that but this has just mixed me up so much."

"We'll find her for you, Cameron. Trust me on that. We'll bring her home." He nodded towards his home. "Now, let's go in, put on a pot of coffee, pull out the cinnamon buns Mom sent over, and start brainstorming. Any little thing, any clue, no matter what, we'll write down and follow up on."

Cameron nodded, his steps heavy and slow as he followed Corbin to the door. In his heart, he knew his brother was helping in the only way he could. He stopped and turned, searching the yards of the houses across the street, his eyes narrowing as he saw a flash of movement and he took off running that way, sliding to a halt as he heard the car take off from around the corner. He was right. Someone was watching him. He waited for a few moments and then turned, walking back towards Corbin, who was heading his way.

"Cameron? What were you thinking?" Corbin's anger came through loud and clear to Cameron, who merely shrugged and brushed by his brother. "Cameron?"

"What? I wasn't supposed to do that? I'm not supposed to look for Carrigan?" Cameron spun on his heel and stalked back towards Corbin. "I'm just supposed to be a good little boy and sit around while others search? That's not happening."

Corbin reached to grasp his brother's arm, holding him still. "All I ask is that you think before you take off. And let someone know where you're going." He ducked as Cameron's fist swung his way and then he just wrapped his arms around his brother, holding him as Cameron wept, his own arms coming up to hug Corbin. "We'll find her, Cameron. Trust me on that."

"I know, Corbin. I'm sorry. I haven't swung at you since I think I was four and you were five? Something like that?"

Corbin's hand on his brother's shoulder directed him into the house and to the kitchen, where he shoved him into a seat. "Something like that. Boy, did both Mom and Dad read us the riot act on that one!"

Cameron grinned, forgetting the present as he slipped to the past. "Did they ever! I'm glad, though, that we have the relationship that we do. It helps."

"I know it does." Corbin's hands had been busy, setting the coffee, finding plates and knives, and then setting the cinnamon buns on the table. "Dig in. Coffee will be a moment. I'll be right back." He returned in a few minutes, a stack of folders in his arms, his laptop on them. "Here's what I've been working on. Your lady has many ideas, you know that?"

Cameron shook his head. "She's kept this very quiet, and I think I know why." His eyes closed, grief taking over for a moment. "She didn't want me to worry, did she?"

"No, she didn't, but that's not why. She told me she didn't like to make accusations without proof. And if she told you, she would be making accusations. She wanted proof. I've found some, but not enough."

Cameron finally sat back, amazed at the information his brother and Carrigan had gathered, but something was missing. "You haven't found him yet?"

Corbin shook his head, his eyes still on his laptop screen, a piece of half-eaten bun in his hand. "No. I should be able to. The name she gave me shows the man died about 20 years ago, but there isn't a lot even about how or why he died. I went and saw the gravestone, talked to people in the town, talked to the retired police chief. They said his car ended up in a lake, but they never could find his body." He looked up at a sudden sound from Cameron. "What?"

"He's not dead!" Cameron rose and began to pace, hands running through his hair before scraping down his face. "He faked his death. But why? He had to change his name. Who would he have bought new identification from?"

Corbin slowly set down his food, reaching for a damp cloth to wipe his fingers, his eyes fastened on his brother's face. "That's exactly what we think, Cameron. If only we could find a photo."

Cameron had his phone out, sending a message to Mark. "I'll ask Mark if her parents have any pictures of him. If he was in school with her mother, then they might have old school photos."

Corbin sat back in his chair, and then rose to refill their coffee mugs. "I talked to them, but didn't go back that far. I'm not sure if Carrigan did either."

Cameron nodded, his attention back on the papers Corbin kept handing him, a frown in place, a prayer in his heart. Just where is

she, Lord? I just want her safe, wherever she
is.

Chapter 20

A month passed, with no word of where Carrigan was, despite searches and newspaper stories and even television reports. Cameron struggled more and more each day, trying to keep up with his work, but spending his off-work hours searching, ending up each night on her front porch, praying he would see the light on inside and that she'd come out to greet him. He slept little and what sleep he did get was disturbed by nightmares.

His parents watched with concern, his mother taking time each day to come in and help in his office. His father had spoken to him many times over the course of the month, but Cameron had shrugged, nodded, shook his head, walked away, depending on the words. Corbin continued to search, scouring every site he could come up with, pulling in favours owed him from friends and even strangers. No one could tell him who the man was. He had become a hidden mystery that no one could uncover. Corbin had privately talked to both Caitlin and Cormac about Cameron and Carrigan, bouncing ideas and plans off them, but to no avail.

Cameron finally looked up one day, his eyes searching for the window, seeing the few flakes of snow that were lazily floating down through the air. His heart was particularly heavy that day. Mark had been by with word that Carrigan's mother was hospitalized, but they weren't sure why. Tests were being run. He said her father was still searching through photos and reports and whatever he could lay his hand on. He had finally been able to produce a faded photograph of Johnson, but Mark wasn't sure even the experts in his department could do anything with it. Mark thought it was their mystery man, but until he could verify that, he wasn't saying much.

Cameron started as a hand was laid on his shoulder. His mother stood there.

"I've finished packing all the boxes for you. I'll head off to the post office with them." Morag watched her youngest son, seeing the devastation in his face.

Cameron had lost weight. Shadows now lay on his face, hollows in his cheeks, blackness under his bloodshot eyes. He nodded, then stood, reaching to give his mother a kiss.

"Thanks, Mom. I'll take the boxes out for you."

She laughed, a finger wagging at him. "Your father has done that already. He said to remind you that you have that do tonight, that you agreed to go with Corbin."

Cameron sank back down, a blank look on his face. "What do? What did I agree to do with Corbin?"

She paused as she was pulling on her gloves, her eyes first on her hands, then raised to her son's face. "You really don't remember?"

He shook his head. "I have no idea, Mom. Again, just what did Corbin talk me into?"

"He didn't talk you into anything. Its that Chamber thing, he said. You have to go. You agreed to go months ago, long before you met Carrigan." She paused, her hand on her son's face. "Just go for a few minutes. Show up with a smile on your face. People will understand if you don't stay for long."

He nodded. "I will, Mom." He groaned as he dropped his head to his chest. "It's black tie, isn't it?" As her quiet laugh, he sighed. "I have no idea if my tux is even wearable."

"I looked after that for you, son. It's hanging in your closet, still wrapped in plastic from the cleaners."

"Thanks, Mom. Are you sure you and Dad don't want to go in my stead?"

She shook a finger at him. "No. You're the businessman. You have to go." She reached to hug him again, her arms tightening around him like they used to when he was a small boy and had suffered some kind of hurt. "God will see you through this, Cameron. I have no doubt of that." She stood for a moment, words tumbling to her lips, that she refused to let pass. He didn't need to hear comfort words, words of remonstrance, words that would just bounce off him.

Corbin stood in the hallway of Cameron's house early that evening, his eyes on his watch. Cameron would make them late and he hated being late.

"Aren't you ready yet?" He called down the hall, knowing that Cameron was almost ready, but unable to resist teasing him.

"I am. I am. Hold your horses, as Pops used to say." Cameron appeared, struggling with a cufflink. "I just can't get this to fasten."

Corbin reached to help his brother, then stood, his eyes on his brother, seeing what his mother had seen earlier, but also seeing something different about him. "Cameron? What did you go and do?"

"What? What do you mean, what did I go and do? Just got ready for this shindig I have no desire to be at."

Cameron shrugged into his suit jacket and then reached for his cloth overcoat. The temperature had dropped and he knew would need the extra warmth it provided.

"You've done something. I can tell." Corbin stood in his brother's way, not letting him pass. "Come on. Give. What did you do."

Cameron stared at him, moved to walk past him, and then stopped, his eyes sliding closed. He reached into a pocket and pulled out a box. "This."

Corbin took the long, thin box, and opened it, his eyes on his brother before he looked down at the gold heart-shaped locket laying there. "Cameron? This is new. What are you thinking?"

Cameron shrugged, an unreadable look on his face at that moment. "I intend to find Carrigan and give her that. She has my heart. She might as well be wearing it." He reached for the box, setting it down on the table in the entry. "Now, let's go and get this over with. I'm in no mood to stay for long."

"Nor am I. I am expecting a call around 10, so I would like to be home by them."

Cameron snorted as he slid into his brother's car. "It's what, 8:00 now? By 9:00 we should be out of there. At least I hope we are. I'm just glad it's only a reception this year and not a sit-down dinner like other years."

"Me, too. What made the change?"

Cameron thought for a moment. "You know, I never heard. It just all of a sudden appeared as a reception." His eyes shot to Corbin as thought crossed him mind. "You don't think…"

"Think what?" Corbin parked and reached for the key in the ignition before he looked over at his brother. "Cameron? What are you thinking?"

Cameron shook his head. "I have no idea, Corbin. Just a bit of a thought that is likely nothing."

"It's those little bits of thoughts that can make or break a case, you know."

Cameron nodded. "I nodded, but it's so farfetched, it can't be right. I'll tell you after. I just want to get in and get out of there."

Cameron greeted friends and fellow business owners, not stopping to talk, something driving him to keep moving. Corbin watched, following closely. He glanced at his watch. Thirty minutes so far, he thought. I'll give him another fifteen and then pull him out of here.

Corbin stood eventually near the entrance to the final room of the mansion that had been rented for the night's reception. Cameron shifted restlessly from foot to foot, unable to stay still, his eyes roaming the rooms and people. He sighed. He wanted out of there, but something kept him in place. What, Lord? Why can't I leave?

Corbin shifted his position, his eyes on the room, seeing for the first time a younger woman standing in there, tight to the bookcases filled with leather-bound books, her eyes on the floor. He frowned. She looked familiar but he couldn't place who she was.

"Are you ready to go now, Corbin?" Cameron's voice carried into the room and caused the young woman to move slightly, bring her profile more into Corbin's line of sight.

Corbin drew in a sharp breath, his hand stopping his brother from moving away. "Cameron!"

"Let's go, Corbin. I've had enough of this." Cameron tried to move away, tried to free himself from his brother's tight grip. "Corbin? I said, let's go."

Corbin was shaking his head, even as he drew Cameron to the room entrance. "We can't, Cameron. In here."

"I'm not going into another room. She's not here."

"And did you expect her to walk up to you and say, "Hi"? Just like that?" Corbin hissed the words at Cameron in a low voice. "Turn around. Cameron, please, just turn around. She's here."

"No, she's not. I've been looking for her everywhere. I didn't see her."

"This is one room you have not even looked into." Corbin shoved Cameron forward.

Cameron caught his balance at the same time he saw the young woman and frowned. She seemed familiar, he thought, as he studied her. She was dressed in a silky red dress which had a tighter bodice and flowed around her legs, just small cap sleeves on her shoulders. Her hair was swept up in a tangle of curls, ringlets and knots. He could see a heavier layer of makeup on her face. He frowned. She really did look familiar.

"Cameron?   That's   Carrigan!" Corbin's low voice had him flinging his head around to stare at him and then back to the young woman.

He walked forward, his head tilted to study her face, which she kept lowered. Corbin was right. It was Carrigan. But what? How?   And who?   His thoughts were jumbled. He had never seen her dressed like this. This was not her.

"Carrigan?" His voice was low as he stopped by her side, hiding her from the door, where Corbin stood on guard, his eyes on the hallway behind him. "Carrigan? It is you. I have been looking all over for you. Where have you been?"

She didn't respond, even when he laid a hand on her arm and drew her around to face him. She refused to look up at him.

"Carrigan?   What is going on?" Cameron shot a bewildered look at Corbin. "Come on. Let's get you out of here."

Corbin nodded and headed for their coats, knowing Cameron would protect Carrigan if necessary.

"I can't." Her voice was low enough that he could barely hear her.

"Yes, you can. Come. Let's get your coat and we'll go." He stopped as he realized she wasn't moving.

"I can't go with you, Cameron. He'll kill you if I do. That's what he said."

"Who? Carrigan, you're not making sense. Let's get you out of here. Where's your coat?"

"He wouldn't let me have one. He said I didn't deserve one. That I had to go out in the cold like this." Her voice was low and monotone, her face expressionless.

"Who? He said what?" Corbin's voice was low in Cameron's ear, incredulous in tone.

Cameron shrugged. "I don't know. I can't get her to move. She's refusing to." He looked around as he heard footsteps coming their way.

"Carrigan? Are you still there? Are you waiting where I asked you to? I have someone I want you to meet." The voice carried through to Carrigan, who shuddered and jumped at the sound.

Cameron gave a low growl of anger and then taking his own overcoat, shoved her arms into it and buttoned it quickly. When she refused to even move a foot, he swept her into his arms and headed for the French doors, Corbin closing them behind them and then running for his car.

Cameron shoved Carrigan into the back seat and jumped in beside her, Corbin barely waiting for him to close the door before he left. He clipped her seat belt in place and then drew her to him with an arm around her. She sat, stiff and unresponsive, not looking up at all.

Corbin finally paused at a local mall. "She'll need some clothes, Cameron. We can't take her to her place."

"I know. I know." Cameron's words were hoarse with feeling and anger. "Can you get her some? And some of that stuff Caitlin uses whenever she's worn make-up? You know, the stuff to remove it?"

Corbin gave a low laugh. "Sit tight. I won't be long. If I'm in luck, a friend is working tonight and can get us what we need. Try and come up with a place to stay."

"My place. It's the last place they'd look."

Corbin shared a look with his brother before he nodded. "That is true. Give me a few minutes. I'll leave the keys. If you have to, take off. I'll find a ride."

Cameron waited, his eyes on Carrigan, a frown on his face, as he tried to make sense of what she had said. Who would want to kill him? He didn't think he had an enemy that desperate. He watched as she seemed to shrink deeper into his coat, almost shrivelling before his eyes. He barely spared Corbin a glance as he jumped back into the car, dropping bags on the front seat, before he drove away. Corbin kept an eye out for anyone tailing him, shooting quick assessing glances at his brother and his lady.

Corbin parked in the attached garage, shutting the door behind them before he reached to open the passenger door and grab the bags, watching as Cameron carried Carrigan into the house. She had refused to move, and neither one of them could understand why.

Cameron set her on her feet, then stared down at them. That's why she's so tall and I wasn't sure it was her, he thought. He reached to pull the red shoes with the high spiked heels from her feet, before he stood in front of her, reaching to remove his coat and throw it towards a chair.

"Carrigan? Can you look at me?" She refused, her eyes on the floor. He sighed, his gaze catching his brother's compassionate, worried look. "Carrigan, I don't think you like looking like this. This isn't you. Here. Corbin got you some stuff. Head into the bathroom here. Take a shower, a bath." He stopped speaking as her head began to shake.

'I can't. I can only use cold water. And I only can take four minutes. That's all I'm allowed."

Cameron stared at her, hearing the sound of anger from his brother. He reached for her hand, pulling her towards the bathroom, reaching to turn on the taps to as warm a water as he thought she could handle before turning back to her.

"Those rules don't apply here, Carrigan. Take all the time you want. Drain the hot water tank if you want to." He reached for the bags Corbin was holding. "Here. We got you some clean clothes. There's stuff for your make-up. If you only take three minutes, I'll make you come back in here. Do you understand?" He waited for her to respond. "Carrigan? I asked if you understood?" At her nod, he sighed. "All right. Just come on back out when you're done."

Corbin watched his brother pace, knowing he would not settle until he could talk to Carrigan and have her answer him. He sighed as he reached for the coffee pot, knowing there would be little sleep for him tonight. He handed Cameron his mug, then turned back to the fridge. He knew their mother had been bringing meals over for Cameron, trying to get him to eat. It was as he thought. There was soup in a container and he pulled that out.

Cameron stilled his pacing, his eyes on the door as he heard the lock snick off and it opened. Carrigan emerged, her wet hair hanging down the back of the bathrobe she had chosen to wear. He walked towards her, stopping as she moved slightly backwards, fear for the moment on her face. He sighed. Lord, I'm in need of some help here. She's afraid and I don't know why. Work in her heart. I know this is not her.

He moved past her, reaching for a towel and then lifting her hair enough to lay it around her shoulders, before he stood, arm around her, watching her face. It was blank, emotionless, and he was suddenly angry. Who was this man who had done this to her?

"Where do you want to sit? Kitchen? Living room? Or would you prefer just to go to bed? It's your choice." Cameron emphasized the latter.

"Living room, please." She suddenly clutched for his hand, feeling as if someone had thrown her a lifeline. "Stay with me. Please? Don't leave me? He'll come looking for me. Don't let him take me away again. Please?" She briefly lifted her eyes and both Cameron and Corbin drew in their breath at the fear, no, terror, that was in the them.

Cameron drew her down to the couch, keeping an arm tight around her. Corbin raised her feet to the couch, tucking a blanket around her. "You're safe, Carrigan. I promise. I won't let him come near you." Cameron's arms tightened around his lady. "Now. A big question. Do you want something to eat?"

She shook her head. "I can't. It's not time for me to eat. I can only eat at noon, only once a day. That's all I am allowed. I can't eat at any other time. I'm not worth it."

Corbin growled under his breath as he quickly moved to fill a bowl with heated soup, find juice, crackers, and then carry the tray to Cameron.

He finally persuaded her to eat and when she was done, tightened his arms around her as she snuggled down on his shoulder, her face turned into him, and then she slept. Cameron watched her for a while before looking up as Corbin handed him a mug.

"Drink that, Cameron. It's some soup, mostly broth for now." Corbin sat himself on the coffee table, his eyes tracking between his brother and Carrigan. "She's been drugged, Cameron."

Cameron nodded. "I know she has. Who is this monster, anyway?"

"That's what we'll find out. I don't think she's been given a lot of a drug, likely just enough to keep her like she is. He's played mind games with her." He watched the emotions flittering across his brother's face. "We'll get her help, Cameron. I have friends who have offered."

"Thanks, Corbin. Let's just go a day at a time for now." Cameron's head went back on the pillow Corbin had tucked behind him and he slept as well.

Corbin watched for a few moments, then cleaned away the remnants of their meal, before finding his laptop and setting himself up in a corner of the room where he could keep watch.

Chapter 21

Stirring early the next morning, Cameron's hand came to rub at his face before he looked around, confused as to why he was sleeping in his living room and as to what the weight was against him. He froze for a moment, watching Carrigan sleep, before he carefully arose, settling her down on the pillows, and went to change from his tuxedo. That had not been in his thoughts at all last night.

Back in the kitchen, he reached for the coffee Corbin had set, looking around for his brother and not seeing him at first. The opening of the back door startled him enough to make his coffee slosh out of the mug over his hand and he grimaced at the heat of it before wiping away the mess.

"Morning, Cameron."

Cameron turned, seeing the fatigue in his brother's face, but something clsc as well. Victory? A sense of finding information? He couldn't quite read him.

"You're up early, Corbin."

Corbin snorted. "I never made it to bed. I pulled the list of the attendees from last night. I think I know who the man is." He sighed. "And we are connected to him. Or at least I am."

Cameron froze for a moment before walking quietly to the hallway to check on Carrigan, before turning back to his brother. "You are? Who?"

Corbin just shook his head. "I've asked Mark and Tim to research him. When I have that information, I'll share."

"That's not good enough, Corbin. Her life is at stake, and if what she says is true, so is mine." He stalked towards his brother, standing toe to toe to him. "So, tell me."

Corbin studied his brother, knowing he was right. When he uttered the name, Cameron's face paled and he shook his head. "That can't be right. No way!"

"I think it is. Now, what about Carrigan? Has she been awake?"

"Not yet. And just why did you let me go to sleep in that tux for, anyway? They're uncomfortable enough as they are."

Corbin laughed at the disgruntled tone in Cameron's voice as he moved towards the living room. "You were out of it, Cameron.

I didn't have the heart to awaken you." He stopped. "Well, hello, and good morning, Carrigan."

Cameron was past his brother and sitting on the coffee table, his hand reaching for Carrigan's as she stirred, his eyes assessing her.

Carrigan sat upright, rubbing at her face and pushing her hair back, twisting it in an attempt to keep it away from her face. She raised her eyes to see Cameron, and surprise and then joy covered her face. Her head was clearer this morning, she thought. But how? And where?

"Cameron? What are you doing here? Where am I?" She was bewildered, not sure of anything anymore, she thought.

"You're awake, and you're looking at me. Last night, you refused to, and we could barely get you to talk to us." Cameron reached for her hands, his warm on hers. "You're at my place. We brought you here last night."

"Last night? What day is it? Aren't we supposed to be going to church this morning?" She watched him shake his head. "We're not? But it's Sunday. Yesterday we spent in Oak City and you made me climb that clock tower." She watched as he continued to shake his head, a look on his face she couldn't read. "It's not? We didn't? Cameron, you're scaring me. What day is it?"

"It's a month later, Carrigan. You disappeared that night. We've been looking for you and finally found you last night at the Chamber reception. We brought you here." He paused, not wanting to push, but knowing he had to. "Where were you? What happened?"

She shuddered before she yanked her hands back and ran for the bathroom, the door slamming behind her. Cameron stood, his hand on his head, staring after her.

"Give her a few moments, Cameron. This is a shock to her, to wake up and find out she's lost quite a few days. Who knows what she's been through?"

"Do we need to get her checked out, do you think? Only I don't want to take her to the hospital. He'll be looking for her."

"He will. I talked to Thad. He's willing to come over and assess her, he said, but if she was more alert today, he thought she'd be okay. When I asked about blood tests for drugs, he hesitated, but said if it was only a low dose, it might not even show up. I asked him to stop by later."

"I need to let Dad know I won't be in today."

"Taken care of. Just said you needed a personal day. He understood."

"Thanks, Corbin." He turned as he heard movement behind him and found Carrigan there, dressed in leggings and a long sweater, but no socks. "You need socks Carrigan."

She stared at him. "I'm not allowed to wear socks. I can only go in my bare feet."

Cameron sighed, realizing she was still under the control of whoever it was. "This is my house, Carrigan. You will wear socks." He shoved her down into a kitchen chair and went to find a pair, bringing a heavy wool pair of his own and tugging both pairs onto her cold feet.

She stared at the bowl of soup and plate of toast set before her, opened her mouth to refuse and then clamped it closed when she was told to eat, that she needed the food, and in his house, Cameron expected her to eat, unless she was sick, and he didn't think she was. They would talk only when she had eaten her fill.

Cameron finally rose, catching Carrigan's hand and pulling her into the living room, shoving her gently down on the couch, before sitting beside her and taking her hand. His eyes on his brother who had entered, a video camera in his hand, he spoke.

"We need to know what happened to you, Carrigan. You were gone for a month. We searched everywhere for you, to no avail. Until Corbin saw you last night, we didn't even know if you were still in the area." He paused, his eyes tracing her beloved features. "Can you talk? Can you remember what happened? Or do you want to wait for a day or so?" He looked around as he heard the door softly close and Mark and Tim slipped into seats nearby. Thank you, Corbin, for thinking of this. And Lord, please, let her remember.

He felt the trembling in her hand and thought to take back his words, even as she began to speak.

"I can, I think, Cameron. It's not nice, that much I know." She glanced up at him, seeing his love for her in his eyes, and sighed. "I really can remember, you know. I just don't want to."

"Tell it as you remember it. Corbin plans on videotaping it." He glanced over at the two officers. "And Mark and Tim are here. They'll take this down as your statement, if you want. That way you only have to tell it once."

She leaned forward to stare at the two officers, surprised but not surprised to find them there, before looking over at Corbin, who smiled at her, even with grimness around his eyes. She nodded as she leaned back, her hand tightening on Cameron's.

"It's okay. Let's do this. But please don't interrupt me. Just let me talk. If you have any questions, I'll try and answer them afterwards if I can." Her face turned gray for a moment and Cameron's breath caught in his throat. "Corbin, start your tape."

When he nodded, she began to speak, giving the date and her full name and address, her face directed at the machine, her eyes shadowed.

"One month ago, I was working in my office at home, late evening if I remember. Or early morning, it could have been. I know I lost track of time. I was researching what had been going on with me, trying to track down a man that I knew as a young girl but who had reportedly been killed in a car accident. There had always been doubts about that."

She paused, her eyes raised to the ceiling, a silent prayer sent up, before she continued.

"I heard a noise at the door and went towards it, when it opened and my alarm system was turned off. Two men entered and I tried to run, but was unable to. One of them caught my arm and kept me still while the other one searched the house. I was pulled out of there, in my sock feet, no coat, and shoved into a car, the man holding me sitting beside me. I tried to reach for the other door and escape but he wouldn't let me. His grip was just too strong for me." She subconsciously rubbed at her wrist, feeling again the pain of the grip.

The men watching her saw as she slipped into the days past. Her demeanour changed and she grew defiant and then fearful and then subservient as she talked.

Chapter 22

Pulled roughly from the vehicle, she stared open-mouthed at the house in front of her, what she could see in the early morning light, dawn just breaking over the horizon. She struggled once more to free herself but couldn't.

This can't be right, she thought. I must be dreaming. This is my doll house. The one I played with as a child. How did it get so big?

She was propelled through the front door and down the hall to an office, what she had always called the study in her childhood. She stared around, fear and disbelief uppermost. What is going on?

She turned on her heel and attempted to run for the doors to the outdoors but one of the men moved in front of her. She stopped, spinning in despair, even as she heard a familiar voice and froze, her eyes on the man who entered.

"You? You're dead!"

He gave a cruel laugh. "No, I'm not, as you can see. I am very much alive. Now, about you, my dear girl. This is now your home.”

“Never. My friends will find me. I will get away from you.” She stood as straight as she could, head back, defiance towards him radiating from her.

“No, I don’t think they will. No one will find you. You’re hiding in plain sight, as they say. I’m a prominent member of the community. No one will suspect me.”

He ranted at her but she shut him out, not hearing his words, just trying to come up with a plan on how to escape. She jumped in surprise as her arm was grasped again and she was walked up the stairs to a bedroom, shoved inside, and the door slammed shut and locked behind her. She stood for a moment, her eyes on the door before she flew towards it, tugging at the knob, trying to pull the door open, and being unsuccessful. No one answered as she pounded at the door and yelled for someone to come and let her out. She finally turned, to face the room, one hand behind her on the door knob, as she frantically searched for a way out.

The windows, she thought, and flew to them, struggling to raise them, only to find she couldn’t. They were fastened shut. She leaned her head again the window in despair and then banged at them, trying to break them and couldn't.

She moved back to the centre of the room, her arms wrapped around her, her eyes searching, even as she spun in a circle, horror on her face, as she recognized the full-size furnishings, duplicates of her toy furniture. What was going on, Lord? Please get me out of here. Protect me. Protect Cameron, please. Let him know I do love him, somehow get that to him, Lord.

She finally sank in despair to the floor, huddled in a heap, her eyes shutting in fatigue, and she slept. She didn't hear the door opening or the man entering, who lifted her to the bed, and then pulled out a syringe, injecting a small amount of fluid into her vein. He stood watching, knowing that this would be something he would repeat every day. He shook his head. It was a job, just a job, but he really was having second thoughts.

Carrigan was roused later that morning and taken to the dining room, made to sit, and watch as the man entered and sat himself at the head of the table. She was given sparse food, just some soup, while he ate a full meal. She stared at him, then down at her own meal, defiance once more raising a head.

When he questioned her, she refused to answer. There was no way she would tell him about her family, about Cameron, about her work. She was finally taken back to her room and the door locked behind her. She frantically searched once more before fatigue took over.

Day after day, it was repeated. She grew thin, tired, her brain foggy. She refused to give in to him, but he was wearing her down. She couldn't think, couldn't concentrate.

He grinned in glee, an evil grin, as he watched her about two weeks after he had brought her to the house. She was his, he thought, almost to the point where she would agree to help him in his work. He turned away, his mind on where he could best use her, before turning back, a frown in place. She wasn't quite there.

Carrigan grew accustomed to her new life, not realizing how far she had gone from who she had been. She grew accustomed to sitting at the table, eyes down as he commanded, not watching as he ate while she sat, nothing in front of her.

She struggled to concentrate, to try and get out of the fog, not realizing that every day, a sedative was being given to her, one that kept her in a fog. She grew thin, white, black circles under her eyes.

She didn't understand as he spoke, but felt the blows to her face and her back when she refused to respond.

Her feet grew cold and when she asked for shoes, she was ignored. After a few days, she asked for slippers, that her feet were cold, and was again ignored. The same when she asked for socks. She was told she had to go in her bare feet, that shoes and socks might damage the floors, and when asked why, when he wore them, she was disciplined harshly, locked up in the room across from her bedroom, a small room she didn't recognize, that had no windows or any semblance of comfort.

She was brought out, stumbling as the light blinded her, and walked down to the study one day. She was not allowed a light in her room. She was shoved into a chair, and the man stood guard, an unreadable look on his face. She just sat, eyes downcast. She had refused to look down at first, but had been beaten mentally and emotionally until she didn't look up at anyone around her. It wasn't worth it, she decided, a flicker of the old self still rising once in a while. How long, dear Lord, how long? And Cameron? Is he safe? Has he agreed to do what he was asked to? Please, dear Lord, not that. Not the boxes.

Sitting in the chair she was required to use, she tucked her feet back, rubbing them together without being seen, trying to warm them up. She sighed to herself. This is my life, now, I guess. Lord, help me. She could not see past the moment, not any more. That was not her, she knew, but she was to the point of giving up, of giving in, of ending it all.

The man stood in the doorway, his eyes on her, cruelty in his look, but also exaltation. He had found the perfect person to further his schemes. He would begin her training today. The reception was only a week away and he wanted a trial run with her then. If it worked, then she would be an asset to his business. If not, then that would be it.

He turned to the woman standing beside him, giving her the instructions of what he wanted. She looked between him and Carrigan, nodding as she understood what was wanted. The doors to the study closed behind her and she stood for a moment before approaching Carrigan, assessing her. There would be work to do, but Carrigan already was a beautiful woman. She just needed to learn how to carry it off in a different way.

Carrigan resisted in any way she could the instructions of how to stand, sit, walk, that she was given, to the point she frustrated the woman instructor. She just didn't understand, she thought. She already knew how to do just that. Gradually, she was worn down and became almost robot-like in her walk and talk. She learned quickly that resisting brought consequences. Talking back had the same effect.

She was unaware that the day of reckoning was quickly approaching and that she was to be used in a scheme to defraud men of money. She would be present in the room, to sit in a corner like a doll, to give a family friendly atmosphere to the discussions the man planned to have. She would have refused, had she known. Her unspoken plea for rescue or, if not rescue, death, was raised daily.

Chapter 23

Shoved down into a chair, her hands placed on the table in front of her, she watched as the woman reached for them a week after she had first appeared in Carrigan's life. She tried to resist the manicure but the guard appeared, holding her wrists as the woman worked. Tears flowed down inside her heart as she saw the red nail polish applied to her fingers. Red was a colour she would never wear. In fact, she knew she never wore nail polish. It was a given with her work that she would mark it up within a day of applying it.

She twisted her hands and tried to escape to no avail. She resisted the hands that worked on her hair, to no avail. The makeup she hated. She didn't wear makeup, she knew, and the layers that were applied to her face appalled her. It wasn't her.

She didn't look up at the dress, feeling it lifted over her head. At this point, she had given up. She had been told she was to wear it and the shoes that she hated to see. She didn't wear spike heels. That she knew. But tonight they were forced on her feet.

She stood, wobbling a bit on the heels, forced to wait for the man to come and find her. Her eyes on the floor as she had been taught in the last few weeks, she watched his black shiny shoes as they walked around her before she felt his hand on her arm, leading her from the room and to the outdoors.

She finally spoke. "It's cold. I need a coat."

He ignored her, until she spoke again.

"It's cold outside. There's snow. I need a coat."

"You don't deserve a coat. You haven't earned it yet. I have a man I am in business talks with. He will be there tonight. I have told him I have a new assistant, who will be there, and who will be taking notes for me. You are my assistant, you understand? You will not talk to anyone else but myself or this man." When she didn't respond, he shook her. "You understand?"

She finally nodded, not liking what she was hearing, fear running through her. Please, Lord? Her silent prayer for safety rose within her. You've promised. Don't let them hurt me.

She shivered even with the heat on in the car. She needed that coat, but it was all part of his conditioning of her, that she was to do without and put up with his training without complaint. If she had not asked, he would have let her have a light wrap.

She stood in the room he left her in, back to a bookshelf, not looking around. She was too afraid to look up. She didn't want to make contact with the wrong person and have that person hurt. She had no idea how long it had been. He had been back a couple of times to check on her, she knew, not saying a word, merely standing in front of her to reinforce his instructions.

She didn't hear the voices of the men who stopped in the doorway, or hear the soft exclamation from one of them. She ignored them, just as she was told to. She started slightly as one approached her, calling her by name.

She recognized the beloved voice, but fear shut her down. He had said that he would kill Cameron if she approached him or was seen with him. That she couldn't allow to happen.

When asked to go with Cameron, she refused, telling him that he would be killed, she couldn't go with him. She had to stay.

When asked about her coat, she just said she wasn't allowed one.

She didn't see the looks shared between Cameron and Corbin, just felt Cameron's coat coming around her in welcome warmth and then she was swept up into his arms and taken from the room, even as she heard her captor's voice coming towards her. She didn't speak, even as Corbin drove them away.

She barely remembered what happened after that, just knowing she was safe. She sighed deeply as with Cameron's arms around her, snuggled tight to him, cradled by the man she loved and who she knew loved her, it was enough. She drifted off to sleep, the first real deep sleep she had had in weeks. At the house, her sleep was restless, often being woken up. And she had been cold, only allowed a sheet at first, gradually working up to a light blanket.

She stopped speaking finally, drained of all emotions, her hand still tight in Cameron's grasp, before he shook her hand loose and just wrapped her in his arms, his tears wetting her hair. She hid her face against him and slept, the emotions of the past weeks driving her to that, to seek restorative rest.

The four men shared grim glances, even as Tim reached for his laptop, to go back over the words she had just recited. It was cruel, Corbin exclaimed, what she had been through.

"Was she the first?" Cameron's voice broke the silence. "Has he done this before? Used young women to bring in business? Or is this something new?"

"From what I understand, no. She was the first one. I've been watching him." Corbin spoke, regret in his voice. "If I had known he would try this, I would have done my best to protect her." He looked up at his brother. "I never saw her with him. Where did he hide her?"

"Johnson hid it well, Corbin. No one knows him at all, I would hazard a guess." Tim looked up. "He's been in business here for years, always skirting just above the law. We've heard rumours over the years but couldn't prove them."

Cameron looked over at his brother, compassion on his face. "He hides it well, Corbin. So does his daughter." He paused. "Where is she, anyway?"

Mark looked up from his phone, just receiving a text message. "She's overseas. I just got confirmation of that. He sent her away about six months ago. Is that about the time you walked away, Corbin?"

He nodded. "I had to. I was sensing something from him that I didn't like, but I couldn't pinpoint. He was using his daughter to try and find out what I was working on all the time. I couldn't have that. It had come to the point that I was avoiding her because of that. I finally walked away. I can't say that she was too broken up." He glanced at Carrigan, his eyes on her face, seeing the changes that had been wrought in it over the past few weeks. "If what she went through is what he put his daughter through, it's no wonder she is like she is."

"What do you mean?" Cameron was puzzled.

"Grasping, greedy, nosy ...." Corbin's voice died away, shame on his face. "I didn't see it at first. Then her character began to come through."

"And that's what would have happened with Carrigan. Does he really think we would not have stepped in last night and taken her away from him?" Cameron's voice had incredulity.

Mark nodded. "That's his arrogance. He thought she was enough under his control that she would have resisted you." He gave

Cameron a grin. "He didn't count on the love between you two breaking that control."

"And it did." Cameron's words were barely audible as he tilted his head to watch his beloved's face. "Now what? He'll be after her again." At the silence that greeted his words, he looked up. "What? Something has happened. What aren't you telling me?"

Mark and Tim exchanged a glance, Mark nodding.

Tim spoke. "Gerry found a box that day, and we'e been keeping it quiet, hoping to spook whoever it was out into the open."

"What did it contain?" Cameron's voice was low, angry and held menace in it. "Tim? Mark? What was in it?"

The two men shared a look with one another and then with Corbin.

Mark sighed, knowing he would have to tell him. "You won't like it, Cameron. I don't think it was meant for Carrigan to see. It would appear to have been planted after she was taken from her home." He paused, his eyes on the floor, before he spoke. "It was a tiny headstone, Cameron."

"A headstone? As in a grave?" Cameron's voice rose in his surprise. Anger burned within him, anger he knew he had to deal with, anger that he needed to give to God. "Whose?" When neither officer responded, he repeated himself. "Whose? Mark? Tim? Corbin? Whose name was on it?"

Mark finally spoke, his eyes fastened on Cameron's face. "Yours. And it had yesterday's date on it. It was a warning, Cameron. He had this planned all along."

Cameron sat, shock on his face, the other men watching him. He glanced down as his lady as she slept, trying to gather his thoughts. "Mark? Is that for real?"

Mark nodded, even as Tim handed over a picture. "That's it, Cameron. I don't know what his plans were, but they are not pretty. We've seen how he worked on Carrigan, and she's a strong lady."

Cameron stared at the picture, seeing his name and the date. "Who does this?"

"Johnson is who, Cameron. He'll go into hiding now, since Carrigan has escaped him. He'll also be looking for you, knowing you'd be the only one who would or could do this, take her from him." Mark shared a look with Tim and Corbin before looking back at Cameron, then down at Carrigan, seeing she had awakened and was listening intently to what was being said. "Carrigan? Would you agree?"

She sat up, shoving at Cameron's arm until he moved it. "He will. That's why I need to leave and let him know I've left."

"That won't work, Carrigan. He'll still go after Cameron. It won't make a whit of difference if you're with him or not. You know that."

She sighed, her face turned to Cameron, her eyes on his. "Unfortunately, he will. He said it over and over, that he would kill Cameron. Even if I stayed with him, that's what would happen. The only thing he wanted me for was to parade around on his arm and fool people. If I wouldn't do that, he said he'd kill me." She looked back at the other men. "It wasn't because of who Cameron is. Not really. It was because of my Dad. He kept saying he owed Dad for having to change his life, for having to hide. I could never figure it out. Then it just became words, like everything else. I couldn't understand, everything was so unclear."

Cameron froze at her words, something in them touching a memory of someone who had been through his shop in the last six months. He couldn't place who it was, but something had been said along those lines. He hadn't been meant to overhear but he had.

"Tim, I heard someone say something like that in the last few months, in the shop. Someone who had come in to get a quote." He shook his head. "I just can't remember who or when."

"Pray it comes back, then, Cameron. That may well be the link we need."

Chapter 24

A week had passed since Cameron had found Carrigan and whisked her away from that mansion. He had refused to let her leave, to let her out of his sight. He knew eventually that would happen, but for now, he just couldn't do that.

Corbin watched them, finally approaching his brother and handing him an envelope, telling him to call him later that night. He needed to open that envelope when he was alone with Carrigan. It was a decision the couple needed to make. Cameron watched his brother walk away, pausing only to set a small gift bag down on the coffee table in the living room, and to say goodbye to Carrigan.

Carrigan watched him closely, her eyes on the envelope.

"What did Corbin do?"

Cameron shrugged, turning the sealed envelope over and over in his hands. "I have no idea, but from his attitude, I would say something life changing for us." He glanced at the door before he walked over and dropped down beside her. "We need to pray, Carrigan, before we open this. This is going to change our lives. I just know it. I have no idea, again, what he's gone and done."

She smiled as she reached for his hand. "As long as you're with me, I think I can face anything"

Cameron watched her for a moment, seeing how she had bounced back as his mother would say. The dark circles under her eyes were fading and she looked rested. He knew she still had trouble sleeping, had heard her pacing the house at night, trying to be quiet and not awaken him. He had laid and prayed for her, knowing that was all he could do.

Finally, he worked a finger under the flap and tore open the envelope, taking out the folded papers. He opened the top one, handing the other one to Carrigan. He barely her gasp of surprise as she opened it, her eyes raising to him in shock.

"Cameron? What is he thinking?"

"What's that?" Cameron glanced over at her, before he became engrossed in the letter. He sat back, a finger tapping it, before Carrigan's hand on his stilled the movement.

"Does he really think we'll do this?"

"Do what?" Cameron looked at her, then took the paper from her. "He really did this, didn't he?"

"You're not making sense, Cameron. Did he really do this?"

He nodded. "That's what he says in his letter. He went to a friend, taking our id's and took out a marriage license for us. Somehow, he had us sign for it. Do you remember doing that?" Cameron's brow wrinkled as he tried to remember, then sighed. "It was the other night. When he was fooling around, remember? He had us signing things, had us altering our signatures, and then signing our regular ones. The scamp. I guess it's legal, isn't it?"

"It would appear so. But Cameron, we can't do this." The shock on Carrigan's face was beginning to wear off. "We can't. You know that."

"I think we can." His hand cupping her face, he kissed her. "I think we can. It may be the only way. I wish I knew for sure."

"We need to pray about this."

"I have been, Carrigan. I've been praying to know how to protect you. Corbin has been the catalyst, I think, God is using to further this." He watched her face as she thought through what he had said. "Don't you see? If you're with me, he might back away."

"But he might kill you still, anyway. I couldn't live with myself if he did that." Carrigan tried to rise, but Cameron just wrapped her in his arms. "Cameron? Don't tell me you're actually considering this."

"I am. Pray about it, Carrigan. That's all I ask." He released her, only for her to stay beside him, her eyes on him. "Carrigan?"

She searched his face and his eyes, seeing he was considering just what Corbin had asked. "You really think we should?"

He nodded, but then spoke. "Only if God says we should. It would be wrong otherwise, Carrigan, to rush in when God has told us to wait." He fingered the marriage license she held. "I'm not sure if this is legal or not, even. It might be." He sighed, his head dropping back as he looked up at the ceiling. "Leave it to Corbin. He knows you can't continue to live here, not like we are. We would need to hide you somewhere, and moving you has such risk."

She nodded, her head going down on his shoulder. "Then what? What do we do? I always thought my Dad and Mom would be at my wedding."

"Then, let's go ahead with it. We'll plan our wedding, get Mark to bring your parents here, come out into the open."

"And force him to out as well? Is that what you're thinking, Cameron?" Surprise, then determination, lit her face. Her love for him was in her eyes.

He kissed her and then leaned his forehead on hers. "That's exactly it. We move you somewhere until that date, or else you stay here and I move. No, that won't work."

She began to laugh, the musical sound of it filling the room and his heart. "You really are confused, aren't you? You have the garage set up as an apartment. You move there. I stay here. Caitlin said she'd move in with me for the duration. We were talking last night, and she raised this very issue."

"So has Dad. I think you're right. I move out there. Corbin said he'd move in with me if we did so, and we'd take turns staying awake at night to watch the house." He began to make plans in his head, losing track of Carrigan until her hand on his face stopped his thoughts.

"One step at a time, Cameron. There's someone you need to talk to first."

"There is?" He stared at her until comprehension dawned. "Yes. There is. I know you're an adult and can make your own decisions, but I need to talk to your father. This is strange. Calling to ask a man you've never met if you can marry his daughter."

She laughed even as she reached for her phone. "You forget. He knows your Dad. You have that on your side." She turned her face away as the phone picked up on the other end. "Dad? Hi? How are you? I have someone here who wants to talk to you. Yes, Cameron. What's that?" She began to laugh. "I'll let him explain, but I pray you agree. You won't? Stop teasing, Dad, and talk to him."

She listened as Cameron spoke with her father, seeing his smile at the teasing she knew he was receiving, finally taking back her phone.

"Dad?"

"Are you sure, love? It's a big step. We wish we could have been there for you through all this." Her father paused, then spoke once more. "We're heading your way tomorrow. Find us somewhere to stay."

"I'm at Cameron's. You can stay here with me. He's in the apartment over his garage. Yes, that's right. It is an attached garage, but the apartment runs over it with its own entrance. It will be so good to see you and Mom. I've missed you. Love you." She set her phone aside, tears sparkling in her eyes, a peaceful look on her face.

"I need to find you a ring now." Cameron reached for her hand.

"What else did Corbin go and do?" She pointed to the gift bag.

Cameron reached into it, pulling out ring boxes. "He didn't!"

"It looks as if he did." She fingered the locket Cameron had given her. "Open them. Let's see if his taste matches yours."

"It doesn't. I hate to see what he bought." He opened the box, surprised at how close Corbin had come to what he would have bought. "He did good. This is one I looked at, but never showed him."

"He asked and they showed him."

He nodded as he slipped on the ring. "Let's pray this adventure is over quickly. I am getting tired of watching over my shoulder."

A week later, Cameron began to pace, his eyes on the back of the church. They had decided not to prolong the time, but to have a very quiet wedding, just with their family, and Tim and Mark of course. Their families had tried to talk them into waiting, but they had looked at one another and each had known the other didn't want to wait.

Cameron's breath caught in his throat as he saw her walking towards her on her father's arm. He would have trouble explaining just how beautiful she was, he knew. But he also knew she would understand. That's who she was.

They didn't see the man who stood across from the church when they exited and ran for the car. His eyes spewed hatred and he began to plot and plan how to reach them, to exact his revenge. And exact it he would. He followed as they travelled through town, part of a convoy of vehicles, until they reached Cormac and Morag's home.

He watched and waited, finally giving in to the cold and leaving, knowing he would find them again, and knowing that one of them at least would never walk away.

Chapter 25

Two months later, Carrigan turned from the door of her office, content, happy, and not worried any more. She had not received any more packages, at least, she didn't think she had. Cameron could have kept them from her, but she didn't think he had.

She looked up as Bill spoke to her.

"Carrigan? What are you doing here? I thought you were out on an investigation?"

She shook her head. "I was, but there was no break-in or robbery, Bill. That was strange. The homeowner was flabbergasted that I showed up. He searched through the house, and came up with nothing missing or no evidence of a break-in."

Bill stopped in his tracks. "Carrigan. That was a set up. If he hadn't been there, you could have disappeared again." He reached to catch her arm and lead her to her chair where she sat abruptly. "We can't let you go out on your own anymore, that's a given."

She nodded. "I think I need a leave of absence, Bill. I'll go work for Cameron for now."

"I think it best. I don't like this, Carrigan. He's still out there, still watching you, still trying to get you back into his clutches. Only you won't walk away this time."

She nodded as she reached for her jacket and purse. "I'm sorry." Her words were barely above a whisper, her tears tracking down her face.

Bill hugged her, holding her tight for a moment, before he set her back and studied her. "You just stay safe. Your work is here, will always be here, when you feel you can return. Even on a contract basis, I want you to stay working for me. Do you understand?" He sighed with relief as she nodded before she brushed past him and almost ran for the door, heading for her car and then her husband.

Cameron looked up with pleasure as Carrigan entered the shop, the look turning to a frown as he saw her face. He shared a look with his father before he rose and drew her back to the kitchen, just holding her until her sobs ceased.

"What happened, sweetheart? And why are you here at this time of day?"

She leaned back, her hands on his upper arms, as she spoke. "I went out on an investigation. Only there was no robbery. No break-in. Bill said it was a set-up and I agree with him. I asked for a leave of absence, until we catch this Johnson or whoever he is."

"I think that's wise. He had to be behind this. He's been too quiet. Tim and Mark haven't found him, not for lack of trying." He turned her back to the front of the shop. "I have a number of orders waiting. If you want, you can work on them. Or you can help Dad with the staining and painting."

She sat at the business desk, immersing herself in the orders, before she paused, a hand reaching out to grasp an invoice and sat, lost in thought. Cormac, watching her and then Cameron, finally rose and walked towards her.

"Carrigan?" He watched as she jerked and then her hand dropped. "What are you thinking?"

"I'm thinking I know where he's hiding. In the house. I just don't know where it is."

Cormac swung a chair around, dropping into it and reaching for a pad of paper and a pen. "Okay, start with what you know. Where were you taken from? Your home, right. So which way did they go from there?"

Step by step, Cormac led her back through her horror of that night, the fear she felt returning until she was trembling, feeling Cameron's arm come around her as he knelt beside her. She didn't see Tim standing behind Cormac, called in by Cameron to take her statement from earlier.

She finally stopped speaking, her words fading as she looked at Cameron, searching his face. "Did I find him, Cameron? Did I really find his house?"

"I don't know, sweetheart. Tim here will look into it. Thank you for walking back through that night. We've been remiss. That's the one thing we never ever did, take you back along the path they took you on. Did they come back the same way the night of the reception?"

She thought, then shook her head. "No, they seemed to go a different route, but I couldn't see. The windows were tinted dark and it was night." She leaned against her husband, drawing from his strength. "Will this end it, do you think?"

"I pray it does." He watched as Tim took the notes from his father. "Thanks, Dad."

"Not a problem, son. It needed to be done. You're too close to her to think of it. It just came to me that maybe we could find him if she could remember the drive." He watched as Carrigan drew herself together and then smiled at her. "You are a brave young woman, Carrigan. I am glad you are part of my family." Cormac rose and walked away, heading for the door, grabbing his jacket on the way by. He needed some time to compose himself.

Tim walked back towards the young couple, a troubled look on his face. "We found the house. It's on the edge of town. We're working on a search warrant now, Carrigan. We need to put you two somewhere safe until we search the house. Once he knows we've been there, he'll come looking for you both with a vengeance. This time, I am afraid one of you will not walk away."

Cameron stood, his arm around Carrigan's shoulder, feeling her unity with him even though she did not know what he was going to say. "We will not hide, Tim. It would only delay the inevitable, won't it?"

Tim stared at his friend before shaking his head. "That's what I told my supervisor you'd say. Carrigan, we will need you to walk us through the house once we've cleared it. Are you up for that?"

"Of course, I am. I need to go back there. With Cameron beside me, I can do just that."

Tim nodded, his attention going to his phone. "Stay where I can reach you. I'm heading out there now."

Cameron watched him walk away, not knowing what danger lay ahead for any of them but feeling it closing in.

"Cameron?" He turned at Carrigan's soft voice. "Go, find your Dad. We need to pray. There's danger ahead, and I'm not sure who will survive. We need God's protection."

He nodded, turning to find Cormac heading his way, stating they needed to pray. He grinned at his Dad as he agreed with him.

Tim appeared later that day, knocking at their house door. Cameron stood back, trying to read his friend, but not able to.

"Tim?"

"Where's Carrigan?" Tim was worried, that much Cameron could see.

"Right here, Tim. Come and eat with us. No. Eat first. Then we talk." Carrigan had appeared in the kitchen doorway. "We have plenty. Morag dropped off a casserole today for us."s

"Sure." Tim waited until the table was finally cleared before he cleared his throat, uncomfortable with what he had to say, but knowing it was necessary. "Carrigan, we found the house. It is incredible how it matches your toy house."

She nodded. "He went to a lot of expense and trouble to do that. I still can't figure out why. If it was to get back at Dad, why do this?"

"Because you are one of the most important people in his life. Hurting his family, particularly his daughter, would wound your father in a way he would never recover from." Tim shared a look with Cameron, who nodded. "We searched the house thoroughly. It was empty as we suspected but we found the evidence we needed that you were kept there. Our team will be spending the next couple of days there. I would like to walk you through it late tomorrow, if you're up to it."

She nodded. "The sooner, the better. I need to do this. Will it be safe? He's still somewhere here in town, watching us, you know."

"We suspect that he is. We just can't find him."

She sat back in her chair, her eyes on the wall across from her. "He's changed his looks since Dad knew him. Dad showed me the picture. He's had to have had plastic surgery."

"We suspected that as well. Unfortunately, without a name of the surgeon, we can't obtain a search warrant and serve it on him." He was frustrated.

"Come and get us when you need us, Tim. I plan on spending the day here at home. We need that." Carrigan was surprised that Cameron was taking that step, but knew he had a reason for it.

The next day, Cameron paced for most of the day. He was uneasy, knowing that Carrigan would be returning to where she had been held captive and beaten down so much. He prayed she would be ready for that. He wasn't, not by a long shot.

Finally, Carrigan approached him, walking into his space and hugging him. "It's going to be all right, Cameron. Trust God."

"I know, sweetheart. It's just so hard to do that." He turned as the doorbell rang, a frown on his face. "Tim's early, isn't he?"

"He is. An hour early."

Cameron hesitated at the door, not sure if he should even open it. He looked through the door window, seeing Tim standing there, and opened the door, stepping back as Tim entered. "You're early, Tim."

Tim nodded, a grim look on his face. "I just got word that Johnson has been spotted close to here. I was told to come get you two and get you out of here. We'll leave for the house now, if you can."

Carrigan ran for her coat, not wanting to wait to see if that man, as she called him, came after her in their house. He had done it once. She refused to let it happen again.

Cameron's hand was tight on hers as they watched the traffic pass by them, a patrol car in front of Tim's car and one behind.

"Isn't this a bit of overkill, Tim? An escort?"

Tim shrugged from where he sat in the front passenger seat. "No. The chief directs this. We have gotten more information on Johnson, and it's not pretty. Carrigan, you came away relatively unscathed. Thank God for that."

"Whatever do you mean?" She waited for him to reply, then sighed. "You can't tell me, can you? That's fine." She sat back, arms folded across her abdomen. "I don't want to know, anyway."

Cameron hid a swift smile at her grumpiness, knowing full well she did want to know. He did, too.

He stood, mouth open, as he stared at the house, before looking over at Carrigan, seeing a grimness in her face. "He really did this?"

She nodded. "Wait until you see the inside. It's a carbon copy, down to the furniture and furnishings. He spent a lot of money on this." She turned to Tim. "He's not going to let me get away, is he?"

Tim shook his head. "He's after you, Carrigan. He's been using Cameron to get to you. We don't think he ever wanted Cameron to build those boxes. It was just a ploy to keep you two together and it worked." He nodded towards the house. "Let's get you inside and then back home as quickly as we can. I want you to walk through, Carrigan, telling me anything and everything you remember. I have an officer here to video tape it and another to take notes."

Finally back in the kitchen, emotionally drained, Carrigan leaned into Cameron as he looked around, the shock of what he was seeing lessening. Tim had moved away, following the officers out to their cars.

"It's incredible, isn't it? It would have been a nice house to have built for you, but I don't suppose you'd even want to see your dollhouse again."

She shook her head. "I couldn't. He's destroyed that." She turned as she heard a noise. "Did you hear that, Cameron? I thought we were alone in the house."

"We are." He grabbed for her hand, heading for the door and the officers outside. "Let's get out of here. I don't like this."

He slid to a stop as he heard the locks clicking in place, and then Tim hammering at the door. "Carrigan? What just happened?"

She spun, fear on her face. "He's in here somewhere. I should have expected this. We should have gone out with Tim. Now, we're trapped." She shuddered as terror came over her, remembrance at what she had gone through surging through her mind. "Cameron, we need to get out of here."

"I know. Is there another entrance?"

She nodded, pulling him with her, finding the door locked and unmovable. "He'll have the windows fastened shut."

"We'll break one and get out." Cameron reached for a heavy brass ornament until her hand stopped him.

"That won't work. They are unbreakable." She spun as she heard the footsteps heading their way. "He's here. Cameron, we can't hide. There won't be any where we can."

Johnson appeared in the entry of the living room, a gloating expression on his face. "You thought you could escape me, my dear. No one ever can. And Mr. Steele? You're here as well. Double bonus, for me." He walked towards them. "This will be it for you both. No one does to me what you two have done."

"And just what have we done?" Carrigan moved in front of Cameron, desperate to save him, but knowing it was likely useless.

"You've driven me from my home." His hand gestured around the room. "Such a lovely home. It's too bad I'll have to burn it now. And you two will be in it."

Cameron shook his head. "I don't think so. God is not ready for us to die yet."

"God?" Johnson scoffed. "He has not part of this. He makes no such decisions." He moved towards Carrigan, reaching out to grab at her arm, as Cameron swept her to one side.

"I don't think so." Cameron lunged towards Johnson, his youth on his side as he slammed him to the floor.

Carrigan stood, hands to her mouth, her screams echoing through the house, as the two men struggled, one on top and then on the bottom. She searched for something she could use, but was afraid she'd hit Cameron by accident. A sudden sound of a shot rang through the room and the men lay still.

Tears streamed down her face as she stood, frozen, unable to make her feet move towards them, sure that Cameron was dead and that she would be shortly as well. She finally moved as Johnson's body slid off Cameron and Cameron rolled away, sitting up and reaching for Carrigan as she threw herself at him, unmindful of the dirt and blood covering him. He wrapped her tight in his arms, burrowing his head against her as she sobbed.

"I thought you were dead. Cameron?"

"He pulled a gun on me at the end there. He couldn't get it pointed at me and pulled the trigger." Cameron's head turned as he watched for movement from the man. "I don't think we have to worry any more."

A sound in the hallway had him spinning as best he could that way, easing back down as he saw Tim rushing towards him, the other officers behind him.

"You two okay? We heard you screaming, Carrigan, and couldn't get it. We had to break down the door."

"He locked it after you left. He was going to leave us here and burn the place down." She looked at Cameron, shock on her face. "God came through, didn't He? He protected us, through it all."

Tim rose from where he had stooped over Johnson, nodding at an officer to send him off for the crime team. "He did, Carrigan. Now, let's get you two out of this room. We'll take your statements, get you assessed at the hospital and then stick you somewhere for the next few days. We have a lot to go over, I'm afraid."

"As long as he can't hurt either one of us. Just make sure no one else can." Cameron rose, drawing Carrigan up with him and out of the house.

Tim stood for a moment, watching, thankful they were safe at last, then turned back, Cameron's eyes following his friend.

Cameron was on the hunt. His wife had gone missing and he wasn't sure just where she was. It had been six months since their episode at the house, and she had been quiet some days. He needed to find her and convince himself she was okay. He finally found her in his shop, her hand tracing the scrollwork on a box he was working on.

She looked up, a smile lighting up her face as she saw him.

"Cameron? Where have you been? I thought you would be here."

He laughed even as he reached to kiss her. "I was hunting for you. I just didn't know where you were. Here you were all the time."

She shook her head. "No, not all the time. I had a visit with Uncle Bill, told him I didn't think I could come back to work, not as an investigator. I just fear going into places on my own now." She shifted in her seat as he moved to sit near her, his hand on hers. "I also had a talk with Tim and then with Mark."

"I thought you might have. What did our friends have to say?"

"Mark first. He said that Mom and Dad were finally able to move around without watching out for someone coming after them. Apparently Johnson had people watching them all the time. Those men have been apprehended and are talking. He really was something else."

"I gathered that. What else?"

"He found Johnson's daughter. She's dead, an overdose he said. She couldn't take what her father was anymore and the stigma attached to being his drove her over the edge. He was a day late finding her. That's so sad. She never had a chance."

"No, she didn't. Mark said at one point, Johnson's wife was dead as well."

Carrigan nodded. "She is." She sighed, her heart breaking for the two women she didn't know. "Dad doesn't say much, but Mom said Johnson was fascinated with her even as a youth. She avoided him whenever it was possible or made sure she was in a group. She thinks part of the reason he went after me was because of that. It was payback."

"More than likely. Now, what did Tim have to say? I know he's been trying to reach me today."

"Tim! Well! That's another story. He is such a character. If I had a brother, I would like him to be like Tim." She turned to watch Cameron as she spoke, finding his eyes on her. "He's done a lot of digging into the past over the last few months. He tracked down the house builder, the suppliers for the furniture, and whoever he could find. Johnson had this planned for years. He faked his death all those years ago, moved to Dad's home town and set up his business. A crooked business by the sounds of it. He posed as an investment consultant, but Tim says most of the money he handled was proceeds from crime. A money launderer, if you will. He found evidence of it in the house.

"And then, there was evidence that he had stalked another young woman, who looked like me, until he ascertained that it wasn't me. Tim said they found all sorts of evidence that he's been following me for years. The bank robbery I witnessed? He had arranged it, but I ended up seeing one of the men by accident. That fuelled his anger towards me even more."

"I wondered if he was behind it. What about all the little objects you have been sent?"

"That was him. He arranged them to come, knowing I would recognize them. And I did. They scared me and almost drove me away from here."

Cameron reached to draw her close to him. "I know they did. They scared me as well. What else? I know there was more."

She nodded, her face rubbing against the soft flannel of his shirt. "He never meant for me to get away. He had planned my death. Tim found the plans. He wouldn't tell me what was planned, other than it wasn't nice. Tim also confirmed that the drug I was given was a sedative, given in just the right amount to get me to the point you found me in. I don't think I can take anything like that ever again."

"We will pray that you won't." He hugged her tight. "Now, what? Where do we go from here?"

She didn't speak for a while, content to be held by the man who loved her more than his own life. He had proven that not just in words but when he went after Johnson.

She finally spoke. "For starters, I will need work. I'm not going back to Bill's, even as a consultant. He agrees, sorry to see me leave, but quite understanding of my reasons. I can continue here part time, but I think I would like to find a place to volunteer. Help women and children."

"Caitlin works for the women's shelter now, remember? She told me they need volunteers and thought of you, but wasn't sure if you would want to."

"That's nice. I'll go and talk with her. What about you, my love?"

"For starters." He grinned as she poked him, a smile on her face. "Right now, I'm content just to be holding you, but work is waiting. Dad's not able to continue right now, not with his shoulder surgery. I know you've been helping him paint and stain. He grumbled that you would be doing him out of work, if you kept up."

"Never. Never that." She was quiet for a moment. "Cameron, did you ever doubt God was there, that He was in control?"

He shrugged. "At times, I guess. The thought would cross my mind that He seemed far away, that He didn't care, but I knew better. I knew He was there and would save us."

"I agree. Even in the depths of what I was in, I knew He was there. He's the only way I stayed sane for that month."

"And I had that talk with Corbin about what he did. He apologized, a sheepish look on his face."

She laughed. "I hope you weren't too hard on him. His heart was in the right place." She snuggled close to her beloved, content and happy.

She finally rose, her hand on Cameron's shoulder. "We need to get to work, my love, but thank you for loving me. I love you more than I can ever say."

He watched her walk back to her desk and smiled. God had blessed him richly, he thought, placing him in the family he had and now with Carrigan. Who knew what laid next. He didn't but he knew the One who did.

Dear Readers:

Thank you for reaching for this book and picking it up. A different read, a different writing for me.

Carrigan went through so much, but her faith stayed firm, as did Cameron's. Faith is the only thing I can think of that gets us through life.

Back in the sixties, when I was six or seven, my father built me a small dollhouse, which consisted of a kitchen/dining room combo, a living room with a fireplace, two bedrooms on the second level and a small bathroom. I spent hours playing with it and hated to grow too old to do just that. He spent time and love making it for me. A cherished memory, for sure.

As I thought of it one day, I imagined what it would have looked like as a real house. From there, my imagination took off and hence the story. When I first started to write, the objects were like game tokens, but that didn't fit where the characters were taking the story, and yes, they took over and took off with it. I, as the writer, was along only for the ride and as a transcriptionist to their story. It happens more often with authors than you think. I had to have a strong woman, who could stand what she went through, and a strong hero to match her.

God bless you as you travel this road called life. Keep your hand in His. It's the only way.

Ronna